Sixty Acres and a Barn

Other Books by Alfred Lewis

Home Is an Island (1951; reissued by Tagus Press, 2012)

Aguarelas Florentinas e Outras Poesias (1986)

ALFRED LEWIS

Sixty Acres and a Barn
A Novel

With a preface by Donald Warrin

Tagus Press at UMass Dartmouth
Dartmouth, Massachusetts

PORTUGUESE IN THE AMERICAS SERIES 4

Tagus Press at UMass Dartmouth

www.portstudies.umassd.edu

© 2005 Suzanna Dutra

Manufactured in the United States of America

General Editor: Frank F. Sousa

Managing Editor: Mario Pereira

The publication of the 2005 edition of this book was made
possible in part by a generous grant from the Government of
the Autonomous Region of the Azores.

Reprinted with corrections, 2012
ISBN for the 2012 paperback edition: 978-1-9332273-9-9

Tagus Press books are produced and distributed for Tagus Press
by University Press of New England, which is a member of the
Green Press Initiative. The paper used in this book meets their
minimum requirement for recycled paper.

For all inquiries, please contact:
Tagus Press at UMass Dartmouth
Center for Portuguese Studies and Culture
285 Old Westport Road
North Dartmouth MA 02747-2300
Tel. 508-999-8255
Fax 508-999-9272
www.portstudies.umassd.edu

The Library of Congress cataloged the original
2005 edition of this book as follows:

Library of Congress Cataloging-in-Publication Data
Lewis, Alfred, 1902–1977.
Sixty acres and a barn / Alfred Lewis
p. cm. — (Portuguese in the Americas Series)
ISBN 0-9722561-5-6
1. Portuguese-Americans—Fiction. 2. Central Valley (Calif.:Valley)—Fiction.
3. Rural families—Fiction. 4. Dairy farmers—Fiction. 5. Immigrants—Fiction.
6. Farm life—Fiction. I. Title. II. Series.
PS3562.E937S59   2004

5 4 3 2 1

Alfred Lewis (born Alfredo Luís; 1902–1977) was born in the little village of Fajãzinha on the mid-Atlantic island of Flores in the Azorean archipelago. Fajãzinha lies only a few miles from the westernmost point of Europe, and it was forward to America that it looked rather than backwards to continental Portugal. A long tradition of male emigration from the western islands of the Azores in American whaleships, and a contrasting reluctance on the part of Lisbon to accept migrants from the archipelago, combined historically to encourage westward migration. Alfred Lewis' family was poor, even by Azorean standards of the time; he was raised in a tiny two-room house built of basalt in the native style. Early on, an older brother succumbed to the attraction of America and left for California. To the classic dilemma of the lure of America versus remaining on the island was added, in Lewis' case, an offer of free higher education in mainland Portugal. These three competing forces were embodied in a father who, like many contemporaries, had returned poor after decades at sea and in the goldfields of the California Sierra, albeit rich in spirit and exotic tales; a mother who sat to the side, quietly praying her rosary and encouraging her son to settle down on the island; and finally, several benefactors who, seeing great intellectual promise in the young man, offered to assist him in obtaining an education at the University of Coimbra.

v

The senior Luís, ex-whaler and gold seeker, was past middle age when Alfred was born. It is not surprising that a regular diet of exotic tales about life in America would lead his sons to emulate him. In his last years Lewis remembered those influences in a poem entitled, "Boy with a Basket of Taro" (in *Aguarelas Florentinas e Outras Poesias*): "Father, smoking,/Story-tells America,/Anew." Add the old whalers who crowded the town squares of Fajãzinha and nearby Fajã Grande and spoke of marvelous, faraway worlds, and it is easy to understand how difficult it would have been to resist the appeal of America.

When he stepped off the train in California, Lewis had only seventy-five cents in his pocket. The very next day, the brother who had "called" him to California put him to work harvesting sweet potatoes and arranged sleeping quarters on a platform above the tuber storage. A series of menial jobs led finally to employment at a Portuguese-language magazine in Hayward and a newspaper in the south San Joaquin Valley. And it was there in the Valley that Lewis would finally settle, marry, and help raise a daughter, Suzanne.

The succeeding years were ones of great transition, of mastering a new language and attempting to adapt to a different culture. Slowly, English became the medium in which he wrote, initially short stories, two of which were referenced in successive issues of *The Best American Short Stories* (Houghton Mifflin,1949 and 1950), and then to his great surprise, a successful novel. *Home Is an Island*—the story of a young boy about to emigrate from his Atlantic island to America, published by Random House in 1951—struck a chord with a war-weary reading public, apparently eager to escape into an idyllic microcosm of tranquility and community.

Other novels followed—never, however, getting beyond the manuscript stage. One rejection slip and the work would be set aside, never again to be submitted, his widow Rose later recounted. For some time Lewis worked on a sequel to his published novel, entitled *The Land Is Here*, the story of young José de Castro, a Portuguese immigrant in California. Clearly autobiographical, as was the case with *Home Is an Island*, the manuscript narrates how Lewis became tubercular—most probably from his nights in the sweet potato storage room—and spent many months in a sanatorium in the Sierra. It was a transforming experience, where he read voraciously the leading American writers of his day: Mencken, Hemingway, Steinbeck, etc. *The Land Is Here*, Lewis' sequel to *Home Is an Island*, is also interesting because it touches on some of the same themes he would eventually develop further in *Sixty Acres and a Barn*. Though somewhat diffuse and lacking in dramatic tension, the earlier work ends with a setting that anticipates his later novel. In the fictional San Joaquin Valley town of Medina, José meets a rich, elderly dairy farmer by the name of Linhares and another acquisitive Portuguese immigrant named Alexandre and his young, unhappy wife, Ana, who ultimately falls in love with the young José.

Borrowing several characters' names and important themes from that previous manuscript material, *Sixty Acres and a Barn* is nevertheless a significantly different work. In *Sixty Acres*, Lewis has greatly intensified the conflict and dramatic tension, much of which revolves around the character of José Linhares, now a good-for-nothing who has brought his young wife Ana from the Azores. And, once again, the young wife and young immigrant, now Luis Sarmento, fall in love. Importantly, Lewis introduces a metacharacter, as it were—the Portuguese community, led by its chief spokesperson, Mrs. Leal—that plays a significant role later in the book. Lewis the autobiographer here retreats into a bit part, that of Pedro Silveira (also the name of Lewis' old mentor in San Francisco, publisher of the *Portuguese Journal*). Silveira is a notary public in the fictional town of Pamplona, ready to lend assistance to needy members of the local Portuguese community, just as Lewis himself had been in the real town of Los Banos.

We do not know when *The Land Is Here* was begun, but Lewis tells us in his "Short Autobiography" (in *Aguarelas Florentinas*) that in 1971 he was still revising it. This suggests that *Sixty Acres and a Barn*, an obvious refinement of the earlier work, was only written in the few years prior to his death in 1977. This time frame coincides with a period of intense poetic creativity by Lewis in both Portuguese and English.

Whereas Lewis retreated largely in his later verse to the idyllic days of his youth, in *Sixty Acres and a Barn* he confronts the themes of human frailty, progress and change and its corollary, rigid adherence to old norms, all of which add layers and complexity to what otherwise might have been a rather banal story straight out of Horatio Alger. While the traditional Azorean values of hard work and thrift are positively presented, most revealing, perhaps, is the underlying theme. In *Home Is an Island,* Lewis extolled the traditional conservative values of the Azores; in contrast, here we see a new, compassionate pragmatism that acknowledges individual circumstance above rigid adherence to established norms. If *Home Is an Island* can be interpreted as an attempt to explain the Old World to the New, in *Sixty Acres* Lewis has reversed the equation as he reveals through his characters the immigrants' need to perceive and adapt to a new reality. While much of Lewis' poetry invokes a striking sense of *saudade* for an idealized world of his youth, *Sixty Acres and a Barn* reveals keen understanding and considerable acceptance of the values of his adopted homeland.

Donald Warrin
University of California, Berkeley

Sixty Acres and a Barn

CHAPTER I

"Pamplona, California," the sign above the railroad station read. Turning

about, he saw a row of drab buildings, of brick and wood, one following the other, quadrangular in shape, all seeming to be of the same size, facing the track.

By degrees he felt disappointed. Had he a return ticket now . . . but this was not the way to behave in the beginning. Action and orientation, he needed both. He walked into the depot and addressed a man sitting at a desk.

"I am Luis Sarmento," the young man said. "Can you direct me to Tomé Madruga's ranch? I've just arrived from the Azores."

The man smiled. "My name is Borba and you must excuse me. I don't speak Portuguese too well. Madruga's place, did you say?" Smiling a little, "I tell you what, you walk to Corvello's pool hall. It's the green-faced building down there. Ask to see the old man. I'm sure he'll help you." Then, after a moment, "And why have you come to California? To get rich?"

"To work, *senhor*." Luis said. "First to pay some debts, and after a while save a little."

"I see," said Mr. Borba. "And it's a fine idea."

Seeing the newcomer standing there, still confused, "Now you come with me," he said, getting up and walking outside. "There, don't you see it? Tell the old man I sent you. Have you any money left after the trip? I'll bet you haven't. Let's see, here's a quarter. Tell Corvello to give you some beans."

Luis walked away from the station after thanking Mr. Borba for his unexpected generosity. Perhaps he had guessed—his total assets were two small silver coins. The money lender had not been too easy with funds. "Just enough to place you in California," he had said. And it had been all right, in a way. He did not want his parents to mortgage all their land for the sake of his coming to the New World.

Walking on, he became aware of the curiosity of the people as he passed them. He saw them smile. It did not take him too long to guess why. They knew. He looked and behaved like an immigrant. He began to hurry, crossing the street almost carelessly.

He recalled his father's explanation a few days before he left. "He'll treat you like a son and, better still, will give you a start in California. I don't think you'll be like the others, going here and there, asking for a job. There you will find one waiting for you, something good and easy, and surely plenty of food. They do things the easy way now in California, I hear."

Luis Sarmento hoped his father's enthusiasm was justified. He knocked on Corvello's door in his best Portuguese manner. He did this a few times and, when no one opened, he walked in timidly. The room had been painted white, but now it appeared sooty and dark. From the walls large patches of plaster had fallen; some of the patches had been partly covered by calendars showing pictures of beautiful girls.

He waited hopefully for the proprietor, or whoever might be in charge, to come to him and ask if he wanted something. But no one moved. There were quite a few men in the room at the time. They sat around a card table and went on playing without much talk. Now and then they banged the table hard, using familiar Portuguese words, real Portuguese as spoken by men of the Azores. Again he recalled his father's saying, "Wherever you'll be in California, anywhere, you'll find someone of our race: you won't be lost."

He approached the card table finally and watched without interest. Then he said, "If you please, I'd like to go to Tio Madruga's ranch. I've just arrived."

"Are you from the island of Flores?" a stout, gray-bearded man asked. "Yes, sir."

The other waited. Then, cautiously, "Maybe—are you the Sarmento boy?" Luis nodded. "Well," the man said in English, "well, well."

Then he went on, "D'you know the old man has been talking about you for months? Ever since your father wrote him. To hear him talk, he'll treat you fine."

"Fat chance!" a player said. "Not unless he works like a horse!"

"And he should," said another. "No doubt of it, you'll sweat for what you get, no handouts. Remember what I say, boy."

"But he'll accept something to warm his belly," an old man said, getting up from the table. "Here, boy, come and sit here, near the stove." Then after a pause, "By the way, my name is Corvello. As one countryman to another, welcome to California." Luis bowed. "They say I can cook as good as any woman," Corvello continued, while he filled a bowl with hot beans, which he placed before Sarmento. He sliced a loaf of French bread, taking, meanwhile, a cube of butter from the icebox. "Eat. Eat everything, boy."

Corvello sat before the newcomer, watching him. "And how are things back home?" he said finally.

"About the same, Tio," Luis said. "Things change very slowly over there." Smiling, "Oh, there is talk of great changes: new, wider roads, electricity, and who knows? Maybe one of these days . . ."

Corvello smiled. "And so you became impatient and came here. You wanted to make a fortune in a great, rich country."

"We had the same idea when we left our villages and islands," a man at the card table said, laughing, "and you may be sure of it, nothing happened." After a pause, "And now we're too old to try again."

"You've got to have a plan," Luis said. "And be willing to work."

"And what d'you call getting up at three every morning? Isn't that work?" was another card player's comment.

"I tell you what caused our downfall, *rapaz*. We were away from everybody on a ranch somewhere, years of it; a little money saved; then one Saturday night . . ." The man spoke softly, without bitterness.

"Let me explain, *rapaz*. What happened was that we couldn't stand it any longer, came to town and walked up to the first *puta* house we could find, Negroes, whites, Chinese, as long as they were women . . . we spent our money on them, then we went back to earn some more."

"Not all of us," Tio Corvello explained. "Some worked, saved, and married, even bought a little land. Is this what you want to do?"

"If Madruga will give me the chance, that's all I'd ask of him," Luis said.

Corvello paused a moment. "I envy you," he said, "so young and eager to gobble the riches of America!" And as if in thought, "I must say it: when I left the island I felt as you do now. It was that hunger for a piece of bread."

"We couldn't breathe, our places were so small," a card player said. "We wanted to become millionaires, *rapaz*."

"At least I'll try to save enough not to worry about the scarcity of rain or too much of it," Luis said.

"That's the way to talk," a very old man spoke for the first time, "and I just know you'll work as hard as you say you will. And d'you know what will happen fifty years from now? You'll be all broken up. Disease will catch up with you. Then they'll take you to the county hospital where you'll die and they'll bury you like a dog. That's what will happen to me and soon."

"Don't mind him," Tio Corvello whispered. "He's been a bum all his life. We're ashamed of him." Luis waited in silence.

"Which reminds me," the proprietor said, "will one of you be good enough to drive our newcomer to Madruga's place? I'd go myself but, you see, I've got to attend to my business."

"I'll give the boy a ride," António Xavier said, as he rose. Sarmento got up, thanked Corvello for his kindness and followed Mr. Xavier out.

"Come back any time. We don't do anything here except play cards and talk—a lot of that."

Mr. Xavier drove along slowly, his truck was old and the road needed repair. Saint George's, it was called, and Luis began to notice the ranches facing it. Most of the buildings were drab-looking, the paint almost gone from the walls and roofs. Their appearance did not vary—a square or rectangular structure, surrounded by a warped fence and a barn much larger and better kept up, or so it seemed. As the truck drove on, Luis caught glimpses of yards, tall weeds, piles of manure and refuse . . . Could this be the California of those postcards he had seen back home?

Mr. Xavier turned to the right toward the range, driving on for a few minutes. "Here we are," he said finally.

The ranch was not unlike the others in appearance. The gate was open, one of its hinges gone. They stopped before the main house and Mr. Xavier tooted the horn, a long, shrill call, and waited. "Does the old man know you're coming?" he asked.

"I think so. But not the exact time."

"He's probably asleep."

The door above the steps finally opened and the boy saw an old man, gray-haired, his rosy face covered by a beard at least two or three weeks old. He was rather tall and erect for his age. "Must be at least seventy," Luis thought, approaching the steps slowly.

"I've brought you a new boarder, Tomé. D'you know who this is?"

The old man waited. Then opening his arms wide, he reached for Luis, and his voice was full of happiness. "You're my friend's boy, aren't you?! How is your father, *rapaz*?"

"In good health," Luis said. "His legs are strong; he can still carry a heavy log on his shoulders, or a bushel of potatoes." After a pause, "And mother is well, too."

"I've never met your mother," Tomé said. "And it's a pity." He spoke to Xavier who had remained in the truck watching the scene. "D'you want a drop of wine, António?"

"No, Tio. I've got to go back." And to Sarmento, "You behave yourself, *rapaz*. Do what Tio says. Don't argue with him. And work hard; he'll tell you what to do."

"Thank you for bringing me here. If ever I can do anything for you ..."

"It's nothing, boy. We're neighbors and countrymen." Smiling, "What's a little ride between friends?" Then he turned around, waved and drove away.

In the house finally, Madruga said, "You didn't bring any baggage along did you? But then what could you bring? What did I bring with me when I left the island in that whaleship? A body to work with, that's all. That, and a lot of foolish ideas about gold and a new place to live somewhere."

Luis nodded, listening in silence. "It was hit-and-miss with me for a long time. Then I heard about California: Everybody was going to that big land out there and I followed the crowd. Soon I was working in a restaurant; no money, just a room to sleep and food—all you wanted to eat, and it was fine while it lasted, and then I heard of this valley and I came here.

"Pamplona wasn't much of a town in those days, but the land around was good. Dairies were being started here and there and I got a milker's job right away, and here I've been slaving, first as a milker, then as a tenant, and finally I bought a tract of land."

Madruga smiled. "They tell me I have the best ranch around and I don't mind telling you I'm proud of it in many ways." Then, "Oh, I almost forgot to ask if you're hungry? You must be."

"I ate at Corvello's, Tio."

"The beans," Madruga nodded. "Good, aren't they? I'm not much of a cook even though I've been cooking for myself ever since I came here. Which reminds me, I've a bit of kale soup left, cooked it yesterday. Come in the kitchen. We'll both have a bite."

"Tio . . ."

"It's all right, *rapaz*. You've got to eat in America. The work is hard; it's good to have your belly full." The old man walked to the wood stove and, uncovering a pot, ladled out two bowls full of soup and potatoes. "I had a few bits of bacon from the pig last year and bones too. Go ahead and tell me if I'm not a better cook than Corvello!" The old man laughed and sat at the head of the rough table watching Luis. "Tastes like the old country, doesn't it?"

Luis nodded politely, thinking meanwhile of those days in his village when he hoped to eat bread and meat every day—always bread and meat. It tasted so good in those special Feast days. Of course, no one could afford a steady diet of it, not even here in America.

Madruga seemed to sense his guest's thoughts. "But we will buy something else, now that you are here, boy. Not only kale, we'll slaughter a calf, a fat one, and who can tell, one of these days I may quit cooking and hire a cook . . . somebody . . . depends on how good you'll turn out as a milker." After a pause, he continued, "And I have plans for you. Funny thing, I've always had plans; they seem to be a part of my life; even when we were chasing whales in the islands of the South Pacific, your father and I, I wanted to come here but your old man . . . There seemed to be a maybe in all that he was going to do. Chances—he took very few."

Madruga cleared the table, then asked, "You're not going to be like your father, are you? Oh, don't misunderstand—he was wonderful in all respects but he just wanted to be sure." He said, smiling, "In America you've got to take risks—risks with time, loans, your own life."

"I'm going to do my best," Luis said. "All I ask is a chance to work. I want you to show me what I must do and how to do it. It's important. I don't want to fail. To begin with, I have obligations. The passage fare must be paid. You see, the money lender back home asked to be paid in a year or less. I'll do it sooner, if I can. We mortgaged our property. I'd die of shame if—"

"It won't happen, boy. Why, I'd advance the money . . ."

"I'm ready to go to work whenever . . ." Luis began.

"Good, *rapaz*! Very good! But first, I will show you your room. Which reminds me, your clothing?"

"A change of underclothes, Tio. That's all I have."

"Doesn't matter, boy. Come along."

Luis followed, wondering where he was being taken.

"Be careful with the fourth step," the old man warned. "It's. been this way a long time. Your feet will get used to it. You put your foot on it just so and nothing will happen. I'll have it fixed one of these days."

Outside in the yard there were tall weeds and, on the uneven ground, deep holes made by trucks, still filled with greenish mud. As Luis walked around them the old man explained, "Five, six loads of gravel would fix this, but I'd be robbed, you can be sure of it. Gravel costs a lot of money in America." Smiling, "And what's a little water pool here and there in winter months? You know where to walk, and pretty soon you get used to it."

Luis saw it at once: the tankhouse was higher than the house and barn. Atop it a windmill swirled and Luis listened carefully to it. It was almost noiseless; he'd be able to sleep while it ran at night.

Madruga looked to the square building before them. "In the beginning there was nothing here, just this and the barn. I lived here, your room-to-be, some twenty years or so. Come to think of it, I didn't build the house. I bought it from the railroad; six hundred dollars I paid for it, a real buy, I thought."

Luis entered his new quarters, followed by the old man and stood in the center of the room in silence.

"It's all right, *rapaz*. The walls are dirty, yes. There are cobwebs all over the place, but d'you know the spiders on this ranch are harmless? I'll get you a broom and you can start cleaning right after supper." Luis nodded. "There's a window broken here," the old man continued. "All I have to do is get some newspapers and stuff the hole. I must warn you our mosquitoes are kind of mean around here, all this water in the fields, you see. But only in the summer months."

Then, pointing to the bunk in place by the window facing the town, he said, "You'll get a fine view from here at night. I used to like that."

The boy thought of his own room back home. He recalled the green, roiling sea in the winter months, how it later took on a sleeping quality:

a sea without breakers, cut by many boats fishing to gather a little food, which was always important in the island, in America, anywhere.

"There's a couple of blankets in the house. I'll bring them in so you can make your own bed." On seeing Sarmento's serious and evident look of disappointment, "Oh, I know how it is. All things look bad in the beginning, and it's natural. But, as I've been saying, you'll get used to everything. A few months, maybe a year, and you'll be behaving like one of us."

Suddenly Luis said, "Tio, d'you have a shovel or a hoe somewhere? I'd like to clean the yard a bit, if you'll let me."

"Let you, boy! Why, you're the first milker ever to offer to do something extra for me. This enthusiasm, I can already see you'll be a success in America! Ah, your father should be here, at this moment. How happy we'd both be watching you taking in stride the hard work." He paused. "Why didn't I marry and have a son like you? But enough of this. You'll be a kind of son to me from now on."

Madruga walked to the back of the house and returned almost at once. "Here's the shovel," he said. "If you don't mind I'll walk up and sleep a bit. We start milking at three. I'll be awake by then."

"I might as well begin by the gate," Luis directed himself silently. The shovel went into the still moist ground and he began to turn it over, slice by slice, in an even pattern. Soon his forehead became moist with perspiration, but he did not mind. This was something he wanted to do. Why, the yard was like a forest! If this was going to be his place to live, at least for a few years (one was never sure) it must be made presentable. His house back home was poor; mortar, stone and tile, but it smelled like a house should smell—of food and fresh fruit in season, and wood burning in the kitchen. Would he in time be able to change Madruga's ways, bring youth and liveliness to this place? "I better go to the tankhouse and sweep my room," he thought, after he finally finished weeding half of the yard. "As soon as the weeds are dry, I'll pile them somewhere to burn." Then a further thought, "And this land is so good, I'll plant a few things, like beans and corn, and fruit trees." Could it be the old man had neglected to plant a peach tree or two, an orange, plum tree, and a few grapes? He must talk to Madruga about this. He walked up to the tankhouse, glancing as he went, toward the old man still asleep on the porch.

His room was swept clean, the blankets on his bunk arranged properly for sleeping. Old as it was, the mattress was comfortable enough. It would not be so bad sleeping alone in this room. And, of course, the old man would not refuse his request for a few necessary things. He'd like a chair, maybe some sort of box in which to store his few belongings.

"It's about three, isn't it, *rapaz?*" The old man's voice reached him from the porch.

"Yes, Tio." It was as if Luis already knew what he must do next. He walked down wearing the same black shoes and trousers which certainly would not last in the work he was about to perform. He should wear what Tio wore, jeans and rough shoes.

"Tio Tomé," he said, smiling, "I want to begin this afternoon; if you're going to hire me, I should be tried first."

"Yes, boy. But the way I see it, I know we're going to get along fine."

"To start with, I need some work clothes. Look at these."

The old man laughed. "Those priest's shoes wouldn't last a day, boy! Walking on wet pavement, the urine and manure . . ."

After a moment, addressing himself, he said, "Why, they might fit! And my trousers, too; he's about my size." To Luis he said, "You go to my room, get into my clothes. Everything you need is there, for now."

"But, Tio . . ."

"Only for a couple of milkings, *rapaz*. Tomorrow we'll go to town and outfit you like a dairy milker, and you need a haircut besides." Luis nodded. "It won't cost a lot, boy. Besides, I'll deduct what is spent from your wages. Fair, isn't it?"

"Yes."

"Go up and change, then. Sure, you may as well get acquainted with your gold mine," Madruga laughed. "Oh, I know. The old-timers told you of those gold pieces all over the streets in any town in California. But you already know it is not true. You can only become somebody by working hard and saving a little."

Madruga's shoes were too wide; the hard leather hurt his feet, and the jeans, unwashed, sweaty, manure-spattered. He was now in the feeding yard, walking slowly among the cows, following the old man.

"A gentle bunch, you can call my animals that, with a few exceptions. The old man patted a large, fat cow on the neck, tenderly. "Her name is Chamarrita, Luis. Here is a cow you've got to respect. Can kick a milk pail away from you without warning. Still, one of my best producers." Luis nodded. "Balbina, this one is called. Now here's a mean one. You've got to fasten her legs as you milk; and here is Gordinha and Cara Branca. Very nervous animals. Still, if you're good to them—it's a question of keeping your eyes open. You do that and you have nothing to worry about."

The cows were coming into the barn. "Do you want to try your hand at a few this afternoon?" Luis nodded assent. "Well, then, help yourself to a milk stool. Have you ever milked before?"

"A goat," Luis said. "We couldn't keep a cow on a half acre."

The old man agreed in silence. "It's easy. Like this: you hold the cow's teat, and pull. Watch me. The thing to do is to hold your fingers together pressing down to force the milk out."

"Yes, sir."

"Press your forehead against your cow and then pull, like this."

"I can do it, Tio," Luis said. "Why, I'll be able to milk ten, twenty cows at one sitting."

"You'll have to do better, *rapaz*. Still, who can tell? I think I'm going to install milking machines in here."

There was great comfort and a sense of intimacy in the silent barn at the moment. The animals were lined up while the two men filled the buckets methodically. All that was heard was the soft sound of the animals eating and the sound of the little white streams hitting the tin buckets.

"I've been coming to this barn twice a day for over fifty years, and d'you know I still like it? My back bothers me now and then, but a good rub can always take care of that."

Two hours later they were done. As far as Luis was concerned, it had not been too bad. Of course, his hands were hot and burning. His forehead was covered with sticky sweat and there was the carrying of the pails full to the milkhouse. He almost fell, trying to avoid a cow backing away from her manger without warning.

"Watch out, boy!" the old man called.

They walked to the milkhouse and washed the milking utensils with great care. "You've got to do this, otherwise the inspector comes along, and before you say hello, he'll condemn your milk, and that's that."

"And shouldn't the milk be clean, Tio?" Luis asked.

"Yes, and I know what clean milk is, but the regulations! You do it this way, all the bugs got to be killed and, like they say, it's all true, but

I ask, what's cleaner than a clean pail or a sterilizer?" Old Madruga chuckled, wiping his face. "As far as I am concerned, old Francisco Barrigão is the cause of all our troubles. The regulations, I mean." Luis waited. "I'll tell you what he did. The crazy Port decided one day to increase his milk output and he did it in the simplest way: he added water. No one paid much attention to this in the beginning. The creamery bought the milk in bulk and arrived at a test by taking a sample from the big tank containing milk from everybody. Barrigão would have gotten away with this but somebody, knowing how many cows he was milking, saw how many milk cans he was taking to the creamery— too many, you see."

"Barrigão was caught, paid a fine, I think two hundred dollars, was put under some sort of watch." Noting the boy's seriousness, Madruga asked, "Don't you think this is funny, *rapaz*? Here's an ignorant Portuguese fooling an inspector, a man of great education, no doubt."

"It was the wrong thing to do, Tio," Luis said.

"I know," the old man agreed. "And d'you know those extra few dollars did the old fool no good? Died a year ago. Sold his dairy six months before; the boys left him, his own wife. He had nothing when he died. Thanks to our Portuguese fraternal organization, he was given a decent funeral. That's one thing about us—when you're in trouble, there's always help coming from somewhere."

"And when we're not?" Luis wanted to know.

"Then we usually wish the smart ones, those who can read a book or newspaper, would do what we do, the work of the farm. We don't respect education as we should. We just don't understand."

The milkhouse was washed in readiness for the early morning milking. "We go up and eat now," Madruga said. Then, "Well, how do you like it so far?"

"It's work, Tio."

They ate the rest of the kale soup for supper. Luis was hungry. He took great mouthfuls of the food, chewing it with evident satisfaction. "Tomorrow we'll try something else. I'll buy some meat," the old man said. Luis smiled his approval. "And now I think you should go to bed. Leave your plate on the sink. I'll rinse it myself."

"Goodnight, Tio."

"Set the alarm clock for three-thirty."

"I'll be ready," Luis said and walked towards the tankhouse.

The lone electric light hanging from the ceiling was burned out. He undressed and lay naked as he was on the bunk, his body hot and tired.

The cotton blanket was pleasant against his skin. The soft wind coming over the Valasquez Range tickled the cottonwood leaves outside. The lights of Pamplona colored the sky with a pink, soft color. Auto horns were heard at irregular intervals, while the steam pipes of the National Creamery whistled on and on, a soft, soothing, even tone. He turned his face from the window and closed his eyes tight, hoping in this foolish way to hold back the tears . . .

The shrill instrument of punctuality was easy to find; the apple crate was nearby and in a moment silence again returned to the room.

Sitting now, he looked toward the old man's house across the yard. It was already lighted. In a few minutes he would hear Madruga descending the steps: one, two, four; he'd miss by habit the third.

The cold air on his face and legs was fine. He rubbed them, feeling the muscles, his hand caressing his feet. Then he put on the old man's socks. He felt a certain revulsion in doing this. The odor of use was on them—the sickening smell of urine and manure. He must stand this uncomfortable ordeal once more, and then he'd change. He must. He smiled, thinking: "Was dirt the price every immigrant must pay in order to be somebody in America?"

In the yard now, he felt a little better; the cool air sharpened his senses, gave a certain enthusiasm to his movements. He walked faster, stomping the ground once or twice.

"*Bom dia, rapaz*," the old man greeted him from the porch.

"Good morning," Luis answered. The smell of the grass cut the day before was pleasant. And here for a fleeting moment he recalled the wild grass of his island, soft and tender, which he used to gather every week for the goat. The smell of that grass persisted in his memory— that and the taste of new fruit and the way the trails went and, above all, the great silence.

"As you can see, everybody gets up early around Pamplona. You can tell the ranches—just count the lighted barns." Pointing this and that way, "Near here, we have Leal's place, and Santos out there. And Isaías Ferreira. António Lucas lives far to the right of us; and there is

Mr. Costa. His ranch touches Pamplona's city limit." Smiling, "As you can see, we Portuguese haven't done so bad in America."

They were in the barn now. The old man climbed a ladder and began forking dry hay down to the mangers. "If you don't mind," he said, "go out and bring in the cows. Open the gate at the end of the corral. D'you know how to whistle?"

"Yes, sir," Luis said, uncomprehending.

"Well, then, go outside the gate, in the field. You'll see the cows out there and whistle. Good and loud. The animals will come to you." After a pause, "And how many will you milk this morning?"

"As many as I can, Tio. I'll take the right side of the barn. If I can't finish my string, I'll call for help."

14

"That's the way to talk," said Madruga. "And I may as well tell you, I did a lot of thinking last night and—but you better go and bring your animals in."

Luis walked to the center of the field. He was at once attacked by a cloud of mosquitoes. Desperately he tried to free himself from them by waving his arms, hitting his own face and neck. He whistled. The animals seemed to understand, and they came into the corral and into the barn, slowly.

"Let's begin, *rapaz*," Madruga said. "Big day ahead of us."

"Yes, sir."

They ate their beans and bread in silence. Then Madruga explained, "This is what we dairymen eat for breakfast—beans, bread and coffee. Some people drink milk, half a gallon at a time. That's why a few of our men have bellies like Turks."

Luis laughed. Tio Tomé caressed his gray beard as if thinking, wanting the words to come. "Like I said, I thought a little about it last night. I may as well come to the point. I want you to stay and work for me. I think you'll turn out to be a fine dairyman one day, the owner of your own dairy, renting some land—a solid Portuguese in California, and you may as well start here. From now on you'll work for me, and I'm willing to pay you fifty dollars a month, always on the first: that's when we get paid by the Creamery." Smiling, he continued, "Isn't it a fair arrangement? It's true you might get more elsewhere, but then what future would you have?" And after a pause he added, "It's up to you, though."

"I'll stay, Tio," Luis said at once. "I was directed to you by my father. And this is a fine ranch. It's true a lot could be done to improve it, but who am I to tell you that? Whatever I learned in school . . ."

"That's the way to talk! You have a lot to learn, you understand that. The hard way, I mean." Smiling, "So they taught you all about dairying back there, did they?" Luis nodded.

The old man masticated a spoonful of beans thoughtfully. "Oh, I know. Old Madruga still uses an outhouse; you go to it, rain or shine, and wash yourself in a barrel, or go to a barber in town. I know all this. I should be buying milking machines, painting the house, getting somebody to hang some curtains on these windows. Mrs. Santos has offered to do it for me. She calls this house a pig pen and, of course, she always laughs when she says that. As for a cook, who knows?" Luis said nothing, listening.

"Now," said the old man, "we better be going to the field out there."

"After lunch I've got to get some clothes, Tio. You said . . ."

"Oh, yes. We'll go to Pamplona after lunch. I tell you what, you may even take a bath. On me. I'll pay for it myself. It'll be kind of a present, me to you, during this, your first day in California."

"Thank you, Tio."

"It's nothing," said the old man, getting up.

The dishes were left on the table. There was no time to wash them and put them away. The sun was already up and above the willows bordering the irrigation ditch a mile or so away.

"It's nearly twelve, boy," the old man wiped the perspiration from his face with a red bandana handkerchief. "Aren't you glad I showed you how to operate our tractor?"

"Yes, sir."

Luis had been initiated in the running of this modern conveyance of the American farm. First, Madruga showed him how to start it, how the mower attached to it cut the grass in even swaths across the field. "You've got to be careful," the old man said, halting the Fordson before Luis, who had been watching him drive it back and forth at a slow, even speed. "Here, take the wheel. Drive on a straight line. Take your time."

Later the old man said, "We'll go in and eat a bite. How about a pitcher full of milk and some bread? There's some left and it's hard, I know. Remind me to buy a loaf today."

Luis nodded. When they had come to the yard, the old man approached the washing trough, "This is the best part of working on this ranch," he explained. He placed his head under the faucet and let the water run over it. Then he cupped his hands and wet his chest, neck and back. "You do the same, *rapaz*, and hurry. We've got to get back by three."

"One of these days I'm going to let you drive the truck. You may as well learn as soon as you can." They were nearing Pamplona now. The old man drove on slowly, getting away from oncoming cars, driving as far as possible on the unpaved road bank. "They let me drive, even though I shouldn't on account of my age. But when you have a ranch and you need things from the store . . ."

"I understand, Tio."

"You know, I just feel you'll be talking like a native one of these days. . . . English, I mean. A word here, a word there, why, before you know it, you'll be an American, voting for Mr. Roosevelt."

"He is dead, Tio."

"Not to me. The only fine man who used to send me a check every month—when things were bad with everybody, that is."

Corvello's establishment was not too busy at this hour. The proprietor sat on his usual stool by the counter, reading the *Portuguese Journal*. About a dozen men leaned against the counter, eating *tremoços* and drinking beer. Seeing Luis and the old man enter, they greeted them, "And how is our green one today?"

"He won't be a green one too long," Madruga answered.

"D'you know he drove a tractor like an expert this morning? Milked a string of cows, too." And his arm about Luis, "Come, I want you to meet some of my friends."

José dos Santos shook hands. "You already know where I live. Come over and see us any time."

"Any time the old man tires of you, I'll give you a job." It was Frederico Leal speaking.

"Welcome to America, *rapaz*," Isaías Ferreira said simply.

"We've got to go," Madruga said. "This boy must shave and get a haircut."

"And a bath. Everybody should take a bath, at least once a month." It was Gabriel, the town's leading do-nothing citizen speaking.

"He's one of us," Madruga explained as they walked outside. "Hasn't done a thing since his wife died ten years ago. Waits until the welfare woman comes over from the county seat, gets an order of bread and beans, enough to last him a week. Then he comes here, picks a chair way in the back, and there he sits. Work? He'd be insulted if you mentioned it."

"Is he sick?" Luis asked.

The old man did not answer. "Anyway, what we want now is a barber."

"Elizeu, I've brought you a customer," Madruga greeted. "Just arrived from the islands. Shave him. Cut his hair. After that, a bath. I'll pay the bill." He said to Luis, "I'll be across the street."

The barber was now beside his new customer, ready. "How short?" he asked in Portuguese.

"Short," Luis answered. He thought of the first time he had visited a barber shop, back in the Azores, just a few days before he boarded ship. He recalled the wonderful mirror, the bottles of many colors on the shelves, the barbers in white coats, shaving, cutting hair with deliberate seriousness.

Senhor de Castro began by asking the inescapable question: "Well, how d'you like this country?" Then his face was lathered. It was wonderful, feeling the towel on his cheeks, steaming hot.

"It's a good place, California," the barber said. He did not expect his customer to answer from under the towel. "Here a young man can work hard, make money and have some fun. How old are you? Not too old, I can tell, so I'd forget about getting married. Just look around, take out some pretty biscuit; or, better still, buy one. It's cheaper in the long run." *Senhor* de Castro paused. "You do like girls, don't you? You should. And with your looks all you've got to do is smile. But, for the present, two dollars is all you need. Better than having some father running after you with a shotgun or something."

De Castro was now shaving Luis, silently, methodically, feeling his cheek as he did so, searching for any not-too-closely-shaved area. "But you haven't, yourself, told me how you like it here, boy."

"Oh fine, *senhor*."

"Even if you stay in one of the oldest ranches near Pamplona? And work from three in the morning to nine at night? Doesn't matter,

17

though. You live with a good Portuguese, and a rich one: money in the bank, land, and the dairy—a man of our race, we should be proud of him." De Castro sprinkled talcum on his customer's face and said, after a pause, "But I don't want you to be like Tio. You've got to live, boy. And I'd demand a few things, like sheets, an electric stove, maybe a radio, and a bathtub."

"I can't. You know, I've just come. This is my second day."

"Well, you think about it, then ask. Who knows, the old man might even be grateful for your ideas."

A young woman walked in and spoke to de Castro. "Soap, towels, and a room change?" The barber nodded. "Here, Conchita, this is Luis Sarmento. Just arrived from the Azores." The barber seemed to be accentuating the words. "This boy is a special friend of mine."

The girl smiled, her deep, black eyes on the young man still in the chair. "She is beautiful," Luis thought, watching her leave. There was something about her walk . . . a disturbing something . . .

Now de Castro spoke of his own success in America: "I've done pretty well, myself, boy. This building is mine. Below, the shop, above, six nice clean rooms, the linens changed regularly. Four I rent; one I keep for myself. And there is Conchita: a girl has to have a place to sleep . . ." As Luis was about to go in the back for his bath, he said, "As I said, boy, whenever you have two dollars, come in and see me . . . Why, the girl will give you your money's worth."

Luis felt wonderful after the bath. That first sensation of hot water covering his body, the soaping of his legs, feet and torso, it had been so relaxing, his first experience in a tub. He recalled the dark room, the small electric globe above him, and a picture of the naked girl on the wall.

"Our friends are happy at your coming," Madruga told Luis later. "It'll do me good, they say and for all I know, they might be right. I'll say it, you won't regret the choice. You will work hard, it's true, but you'd have to do that wherever you went, and at no better pay. Then, your future, we will talk about that one of these days."

"Yes, Tio," the boy answered listlessly. He was thinking of the years ahead, in this drab group of buildings set in a flat alfalfa field dotted by clumps of willows.

"It's good to be back," Madruga said, driving in the yard. "D'you know this place already looks different? The cleaning, you see . . ."

"But there's a lot more to do, Tio. The land back of the house, for instance: why not spade it and plant a few vegetables?"

"Like peppers and tomatoes?"

"Yes."

"And taro? I remember eating it with broiled fish in the Kanaka Islands. Me and your father. Oh, we had fine times in those days!"

"You'll see how good a gardener I am, Tio." Luis was thinking of what he used to plant at home. "Even potatoes, we used to grow everything in a small *nisca* of ground. We had to. Plant and plant again." Looking at the plot of rich soil before him, "Why, it's a sin to let it stay idle! A mortal sin, Tio."

"Which reminds me, we have a Portuguese priest in Pamplona. A fine man, whom I'm sure you will want to meet."

19

One of his best friends, Luis recalled, had been Father Cordeiro. It was he who had told him about America, the real truth about it, without embellishments. A land of great opportunities where one could advance fast or slow, one's ambition being the measuring stick. He recalled this last statement especially. They were at the seashore listening to the sea.

"Out there," the priest had a habit of repeating his words. "Out there, there is the answer. If you are restless, if you want more than you find in your village . . .

"Next Sunday, Tio," Luis said. "We'll go to church together, and . . ."

"Oh, oh, *rapaz*, I must tell you something. D'you know I haven't been to church, let's see, in thirty, forty years?"

"Why?" Luis wanted to know. "At least as a means to meet your friends. My father used to say he felt good inside whenever he went."

"Oh, the truth is, *rapaz*, I don't really know why I haven't gone. As far as I can see, it's the work. You work like a horse, fourteen hours a day, and then, Sunday is different, you see. Just the milking, no more. You want to lie around and sleep. Myself, I don't even go to Corvello's, and you can be sure not to de Castro's either."

"How about this Sunday, Tio? You and I?"

The old man shook his head. "Go by yourself, boy. Which reminds me, I've bought an extra pair of jeans and a shirt for you. A kind of present."

"Thank you, Tio."

This was his third milking and he felt better. His hands were not swollen, nor the fingers; he seemed to have a certain knack for the work. Instinctively, he had learned to do his chores: to get up at three, go to the field to bring in the cows, milk his share of them. There was no choice of the cows; he found gentle and unpredictable animals. He knew his days would be alike, no variation in the toil nor the manner of doing it. Still, there would be happy hours now and then—attending church or taking a bath in de Castro's barbershop.

He felt so different in his blue jeans and shirt this afternoon. The smell of America was in these garments, a clean, pleasant smell, and he promised himself that he would wash his garments regularly—a bar of soap and a little rubbing, an easy thing to do.

Madruga's voice reached him from the other side. "How're you doing, *rapaz*?"

"All right, Tio."

"I forgot to tell you, while you were at the barber's I walked to the butcher shop and bought some meat. How about you and me cooking a little beef stew this evening?"

"Oh, yes, Tio!" Luis said, his fingers pulling methodically on the cow's teats. Back home, whenever his family could afford to buy a little meat, it usually turned out to be a feast day in the house. His mother would ask him to come in the kitchen to "help" her and he would peel new potatoes when in season. Then onions and herbs would be added to the meat, and the known, wonderful smell would call the neighborhood's attention to what was being cooked in his house. The men, recognizing the smell, would speak of America, that big land where everyone could have not only meat and eggs but chicken itself, not to mention white bread and butter. Hunger was unknown over there . . .

Luis carried the pailful of milk to the milkhouse, dropping a little on the cement floor for the waiting cat. Later, in the kitchen, the old man unwrapped the package of meat, placing the medium-sized cubes in a steel pot. The dry cottonwood burned fiercely—the old man himself had cut it to size to fit the stove. "You must know I don't cook this too often. I just thought—you're young, you see."

It was nearly dark when they ate. Luis was hungry. This was his first abundant meal in America and he was grateful to the old man. "A woman cook couldn't have done better, Tio."

"Oh yes, any woman could. I may as well tell you, after your stay here, say, two or three months, I'll make a few changes. First, I'll buy another string of cows. Then I'll hire a milker, a married one, and his wife will be our cook—which reminds me: out of your fifty dollars, you must save at least forty. Let's see, the passage fare cost you how much?"

"Two hundred and fifteen, Tio."

The old man said, "The way I figure, you ought to pay it in about five months. You won't be broke during this time."

"It's true, Tio."

"That is as it should be. You will have to have a little spending money to get a haircut once in a while. I'd buy a razor and shave." The old man laughed. "D'you know, *rapaz*, if you keep away from those ladies de Castro offers to everybody, you may even be able to save your own spending money?"

Again he had washed the tankhouse room. He had swept the floor clean, dusted the walls and ceiling, even the steps. No vestige of manure must be left there. Tonight, after that fine meal, he felt good lying on his bunk, naked as usual, watching the night unroll its darkness over the countryside, and over Pamplona itself, so humble during the day and now so lovely and mysterious under the throbbing neon lights.

Watching it, he felt the first pangs of loneliness, a strange indefinable hunger, which the work of the ranch and a good future hinted by Madruga did not seem enough to contain.

The desire to leave one evening, perhaps a visit to Corvello's place or a walk up and down Main Street . . . that girl on the calendar in de Castro's bathroom beckoned to him now. He recalled her in minute detail. Then he thought of his milking chore at three-thirty. He checked the alarm, winding it. Then his legs traveled under the blanket to the coolest spot and he lay still; finally he slept.

21

"It's like a red barn," Madruga had described Saint Sebastian's Church to Luis, "except that it has a high steeple topped by a white cross. When you're in there, watch for the stained glass windows. I gave the church one of those, the one in the back, on the right side, closest to the entrance."

Luis sat on a bench listening to the priest's sermon. He must be the one Madruga had mentioned. He wondered why he, too, had come to America. What had caused him to leave? Was it personal ambition, the hope of a fine church appointment, the leadership of a Portuguese colony somewhere, or was it mere wanderlust? Had he, too, been the victim of those wonderful tales heard back home?

The priest said that heaven was always a certainty, honest work the means of subjugating one's lustful flesh. "Remember your past," he said. "It must be kept alive as a never-burning star. It represents a good, wholesome life and your dear ones back there, write to them; send them a gift of money, or clothes, anything."

As Luis came outside after Mass, a group of his countrymen formed a circle around him. He was asked the usual questions: The quality of the crops this year? Had there been enough rain? Were the roads paved? They had heard an automobile could go around the island, was this true? And he was invited to visit their homes. They lived nearby. All he had to do was drive along Saint George's Road. And, they said, "You stay with Tio Tomé. He's old, he'll die one of these days, and he's rich, worth at least two hundred and fifty thousand! Made it all himself!"

He walked away under the willow-covered street. That last statement—A quarter of a million dollars! Earned by one man! Was it true? If Tio Tomé had done this, why he himself could . . . in a matter of weeks he'd be receiving his first pay, and after that . . . for one thing, he liked the work. Why, getting out of bed at three wasn't too bad. It was good to go out in the dark with all that silence around, the feel of the grass so cool against his legs as he walked through it . . .

Pamplona's main street was almost deserted on Sundays. Store windows featuring hardware, groceries and ladies' dresses appeared as if abandoned, collecting dust under the warm sunlight. As he walked on slowly, almost aimlessly, he passed bearded men carrying bundles on their backs. Now and then a car drove by, sounding loud, almost out of place at that hour.

Corvello's place seemed to be the only establishment where people were to be found. He could tell by the number of automobiles parked before it. He walked fast as he passed de Castro's shop. He wondered where the barber was—perhaps in his room. Should he walk up and say hello? No, temptation must be fought by means of hard work, more and more of it. Yes, he must stay on the farm, unless . . . This resolve was tainted. He hadn't yet been paid.

One morning Madruga called him to the kitchen. "*Rapaz*, he said, "d'you know what day this is?" Luis waited. "It's pay day! *Pay day!*" Madruga accentuated. "You must learn this word. Never forget it. Payday is the most important day in America. I must pay you for what you've done."

"Thank you, Tio."

"You've earned every cent, boy. Look at the yard outside. Spaded, vegetables already growing. I will say you have brought life to this place. I am very happy." The old man dug into his trousers back-pocket and brought forth a wallet. Then he counted a few bills, feeling each one as he did so and placed them on the table. "Count your money, boy."

His first earned money! If only his father were here now! Or some of the girls who had refused to take him seriously. After all, when one is about to leave, how is one to know when, if ever, one will return? Fifty dollars! Think of it!

"If I were you," Madruga said, "I'd put this money away where it will be safe. I'd even start an account in your name at the bank right away. We could drive to Pamplona this afternoon."

"Yes, sir."

"Go ahead. Feel the bills. They're good to touch, eh?" Smiling, "In the old days, it was gold. Twenty-dollar pieces. That's how I paid for this ranch. With gold." After a pause, "But things change, and we've got to go with the times. Pretty soon we'll have the milking machines and we already have a tractor. Remember that first day? It was fine driving it, wasn't it?" Luis nodded.

"I am glad you decided to modernize the ranch, Tio. Tell me, what made you buy the tractor? There aren't too many around, the way I see it."

"Not yet," the old man agreed. "I will tell you what happened: the owner was in trouble. Couldn't pay for it, and so I took it off his hands, for a reduced price. You've got to watch for bargains like that in America."

Tio Madruga seemed to be well-known at the bank. As he came in, Mr. Romano, the manager, greeted him. "Hello, you old Port, and how many thousands will you leave with us this morning?"

The old man laughed. "Not this time," he said. "When you pay a little more interest I'll be tempted to dig under the house and bring along an old can. You'd like that, eh?" And then he said, after a moment, "Oh, by the way, I'd like you to meet Luis Sarmento. Just arrived from the Old Country."

"Another milker," Mr. Romano said smiling.

"That's right," Madruga said. "I want you to give him good counsel. Tell him to save his money, to be smart . . . when he speaks English, that is."

"I'll do that," Mr. Romano said, pumping Sarmento's hand.

"I thought he should open an account with you, deposit his first month's wages, less ten dollars. D'you think this is a good idea?"

"Yes," Mr. Romano said, returning to his desk followed by Luis and Madruga. "Who knows? This boy may be as rich as you one day."

"I hope so," the old man said. "I'd like to live long enough to see him succeed at least in a small way. It takes time to get to the top."

"That's right," Mr. Romano agreed, filling out a small card which Luis was asked to sign.

The manager examined Sarmento's signature. "This one writes well." He quickly added, "But if you have brains, what if one does use a cross as signature. Like I said, brains."

"Hard work, don't forget that," said the old man.

The banker waved to another waiting client, saying "I'll be with you in a minute," a sign that the interview with Madruga and his protégé was over. Outside, the old man said, "This is how business is done in

America, boy. You go to the bank and deposit some money. Then, if you don't spend it and keep on adding to the pile, as much and as often as possible, you'll soon find yourself worth something. When this happens you'll have what they call credit. Then you can borrow more than you have put away: enough for a down payment on a share of my dairy." The old man rubbed his beard slowly. "Too soon, boy. There's the passage fare to pay first."

They were now before Corvello's pool hall. "We could go in and eat a bowl of beans, boy. What d'you say?"

"A good idea, Tio," Luis said. "But under one condition. Today I have ten dollars. We'll eat at Corvello's, but I'll pay for our lunch. Can you imagine, Tio—why, I can treat a friend, buy something! I can even deposit a coin in the church basket. This is wonderful!"

"You shouldn't be too free with it. Remember how hard it was to earn your first dollars. One full month, milking twice a day, hay-cutting, irrigating . . ."

"I know, Tio. Still, what's the point of having money if you can't share it, a little of it at least, with friends?"

This was the day after the bi-monthly milk payment by the Dairy Producers Association. Every Portuguese was in town. They came to Pamplona to cash their checks and pay their current bills. Pamplona owed most of its progress to the owners of small ranches, thirty- and sixty-acre tracts. The Portuguese supported to a great extent their churches, implement dealers, grocery stores. "We don't talk too good and we bargain a little, that's our way; but in the end we buy. Our kids have to eat."

As Madruga and Luis came in, Corvello's place was crowded. All tables were occupied except a few stools by the corner.

"Bring us some food," Madruga ordered, "and don't be stingy with the bread, and it better be fresh."

Corvello wiped the counter before them, then proceeded to fill two bowls with beans, slicing half a loaf of bread meanwhile. "If this isn't enough, call me," he said.

"How d'you like America, boy?" It was the same oft-repeated question. "Been here a month, haven't you?" a dairy hand asked. "Aren't you ready to go back?"

"Not yet," Luis said curtly.

"All by yourself, working like a donkey, going nowhere. Why don't you come to town at night now and then? You should . . ." he said laughing, "but you may have your own favorite heifer calf already." Luis did not understand.

Madruga said, "Is this what you do, Mateus? I'd like to tell you, this boy doesn't do sinful things like that." Hesitating a moment, he said, "If he wants a woman there's always someone, even though two dollars is a lot to pay for something such as you have in your filthy mind."

"I'm only joking, Tio."

"You let this boy stay the way he is. For a little while, at least."

Even the women were concerned about him, Luis thought, eating his food in silence. A few days before *Senhora* dos Santos had called him over for a cup of coffee. "You can't go on like this," she had said. "You should look around; a fine young girl, a young couple could bring new life to the old man's place."

"That's right, neighbor," Mrs. Leal had said, walking in. "I saw our new young man coming to your house, so I thought I'd drop in and have a sip of coffee with you."

"Yes, Maria, I was saying Luis should marry soon. It's foolish to wait until you're rich, for then who'd want to suffer an old man's complaints, tend his sickness?"

There had been a pause, during which Mrs. Leal had glanced toward the door. It was another neighbor, Mrs. Ferreira, who offered at once her own excuse for coming. "I just had to know—how are things back in my island?"

Luis smiled, remembering this. Madruga said, "I'm going to the butcher's to buy some meat. How about a roast, a nice, tender one? Just enough for us, and if there's any left we'll finish it the next day."

The boy nodded. "I think I'll go to de Castro's for another haircut, Tio."

"You do that."

"Oh! Oh!" the barber greeted him. "How d'you like . . ."

"Stop it, Tio. Yes, I like it very much."

De Castro laughed. "Oh, I know how you feel. The truth is, all of us have answered the same questions before. It's only natural with our people. We're really curious and, of course, the idea of you and the old man together, a rich, rich man—he may not live too long, you see." Quickly he added, "Not that I wish it."

27

The customer in the chair had his face powdered, his hair brushed, and when he left the shop the barber said, "You're next, boy."

There was silence during the entire hair-cutting process. Then de Castro asked, "I suppose you got paid today."

"Yes. It's all in the bank, except ten dollars."

De Castro said, "Ten dollars, eh?" Luis nodded.

"Enough to go to the movies. We could, one of these days. Ever been?"

"No," the boy said.

The barber looked about furtively, as if someone might secretly be near. "What I really mean is, why don't you come down this evening? This is your first payday. Why, I'd really make a night of it! And, yes, that girl just came from the doctor this afternoon—she's clean. You come on up: I'll take you to her myself." He smiled. "Funny thing, she was asking about you today. 'That Portuguez,' she said, 'I'd like to see him and talk to him about my Mexico.' She comes from a place near the coast, Sinaloa, I think."

Luis waited. De Castro was apologetic about it. "It's the idea that I don't want you to suffer, boy. Here you've been a whole month, and nothing! Don't you think you owe it to yourself? You should thank me, really."

Luis got up from the chair. The strange words from this man excited him. He was trembling a little. "I think I'll take a bath," he said.

He wasn't too hungry this evening, he told Madruga. The roast could wait, tomorrow would be just fine; it was too hot to be around the stove anyway.

"In that case," said the old man, "how about the kind of supper I really like, milk and bread, I mean? The loaf was still hot when I bought it this afternoon." Luis nodded. "We'll fill our bowls, dump the bread in the milk and let it stay until the crust is really soft . . . Man!"

"I think I'll walk to town this evening, Tio. Mr. de Castro is taking me to a movie. I've never seen . . ."

The old man waited, thinking, "Neither have I," he said. "Not even when they show our lands back there, and I suppose it's all right." Then, suddenly, he said, "Are you sure it's the movies? Will you tell me about it when you come back?"

"I will, Tio."

The old man smiled. "Remember, the ten dollars will have to last you four weeks. You understand that?"

"Yes, sir."

"I should forbid you to go out, really. It's too early to begin. There's plenty of time for shows, pool halls and other pastimes. I am, in a way, responsible for your behavior and . . ."

"I'll be careful, Tio."

The old man did not answer. He got up and began to clear the table. "Go," he said. "You should be back before ten."

Anyway, he told himself, walking to Pamplona, this was one of the reasons why he had come to America. It was one point the ancients of his village made clear: the women were beautiful; easy to find. Why, they hadn't been in California a week when . . . It had been as easy as that.

He was fifteen or thereabout when he had been allowed to listen to these tales of discovery. He recalled his first curiosity and desire: there was one girl, he was content to look at her, and whenever she smiled at him, he did great things like carrying an extra load of wood on his back, much to his father's amusement. Oh, she was so beautiful! And when that American arrived, a big man who dressed well and wore cologne, she agreed to marry him and in due time left the village, never to return. They were to live in New Bedford, somewhere outside of California.

That girl had been his first love. He remembered her leaving the village, so small beside that giant of a man. And now here he was seeking that release which contact with a woman may bring. As he approached Pamplona he began to feel uneasy, became self-conscious, as if the whole town already knew what he was about to do.

It was a quarter-past-nine when he walked by the theater. The bright lights were still on. A girl sat in a glass cage in front, waiting. She became attentive as he approached. He looked at the various posters advertising the show, saw a beautiful girl being kissed by a man well-groomed, with dark and glossy hair. This poster helped to disturb him. A boy came out escorting a girl, his arms knowingly about her, their hips touching. He watched them get into a car and drive away into the night . . .

"At least I can go up and talk to de Castro," he told himself, walking away. As he approached his outside door, he looked up and down to see if anyone was watching. Once inside, he became conscious of a strong lotion smell which he thought came from his friend's room. The barber responded to his knock almost at once, greeting him in baggy trousers, slippers and undershirt.

"Oh! It's you, boy. I suppose you came to visit the girl. Good. This seems to be a quiet night. Nobody around. You can stay an hour with her if you care to." And all business now, "You wait here a minute."

De Castro shuffled to the door at the end of the corridor and knocked. It was opened almost at once. "It's all right, boy. Come." In a lower voice, he said, "You do your best. Show her you're no greenhorn. She'll like that. Oh yes, d'you have two dollars? Maybe four? Conchita has to eat."

He stood in the center of the room, knowing he must appear rather foolish to this girl who, without a word, latched the door and turned out the light. He guessed the reason why. From the theater marquee enough light would come in through the open window, soft yellow, blue and green . . .

"You want to see Concha, yes?" The girl had a certain directness about her. "Give me two dollars then."

Luis, still embarrassed, watched her undress. "You," she said, "go on. Take off your own clothes."

He was clumsy unbuttoning his shirt and Concha approached him. "Let me," she said. He felt her fingers wander on his chest, professionally. "Come," she said, "you want to talk to me, no?" She kissed him on the mouth, a long, intriguing kiss. He was now all confusion, lying beside her on the bed. "You want to tell me about yourself? What's your country like?"

It was then that he thought of the girl back home, his first love. She, too, had thrilled him, without physical contact. Where was she at this moment? Were her lips as exciting as this girl's as she lay naked by his side?

"There is little to say." Luis was glad of this chance to talk. "I left my father and mother. They're out there by themselves, no brother or sisters. As for my island, it is very poor. That's why I came here."

Now her hands wandered again. "You want a lot of love, don't you?" She turned on her side, smiling, facing him. It was then he began to respond to her caress. She was like warm water running all over his body. His fingers tingled with a delightful urgency. Now he thought he did not have enough passion to give. He went into her avidly, wanted to stay with her in this way forever. When release came, he rolled back, his arms still around her, all the words gone from his mouth.

"I better go back," he said after a while.

Concha remained silent a few moments. Then she said, "Stay a while longer. We'll talk some more."

"I've got to be up at three," Luis explained. "Milking and everything. We're very busy now."

"I wouldn't ask you for money."

"I will come back." He was dressing calmly before her. Still naked, Concha followed him to the door and unlatched it. Suddenly, she said, pressing her body to his, "Tomorrow, yes?"

They had spoken in Spanish and Portuguese, yet they had found no difficulty in understanding each other. More important than the spoken word, Luis thought, had been the strange initiation, and now this wonderful peace and comfort.

In the distance he saw the ranch, the single electric globe delineating it in the great peace and coolness of the evening. Madruga would probably be sitting on the porch, rocking away. Should he tell him what had happened?

No. He'd go to his room and sleep. Anyway, the old man already knew, or guessed where he had been . . .

Dear Mother and Father . . . Before him, on the kitchen table lay a
paper pad and a bank draft for two hundred and fifty dollars. This sum
represented a first phase of his life in America—a time of exchange of
what Luis knew and loved for the strange and untried. He recalled his
first week, the second and the one after that, and his first serious talk
with Madruga a few weeks after. It had taken place at this same table;
the stillness of summer was everywhere; a breeze cool and smelling of
cut alfalfa came in the room in small, tingling waves.

The old man had started the conversation. "Many people would
like to put me on the retired list, an old man ready to buy a house
somewhere near the seashore, maybe Monterey or Santa Cruz. They
would like to see me playing cards under a cypress, something pleasant
and easy to pass the time away."

Luis had answered at once. "No one can retire, Tio. I see it this way:
maybe you slow up a little but you go on. Leave this ranch? You really
can't. It's a part of you. You know everything about it, know everyone
in our colony."

He recalled Madruga's startled expression, hearing him talk this way.
"Not only a good worker, boy, you also have a clear thinking head."

"One has to, Tio," he had said. "There's a certain pleasure in the
making of a fortune, little or much of it, I've discovered. Why those
first fifty dollars . . ."

He remembered the old man's laughter then. "I know, I know, boy.
And don't give it a further thought—I'm staying. As long as I know
you are happy living here with me." After a pause, he said, "You are,
aren't you?"

"I am, Tio," he said. He remembered thinking that now was the time to discuss it. "Which reminds me, may I ask . . ."

"What, boy? And how much will it cost?"

"The cost is up to you, Tio," he had said. "What I mean is, the time is here when you should show our neighbors that you're progressive."

"I have," the old man said. "We already have the tractor, haven't we?" This was a rather evasive answer. He recalled the old man rubbing his beard vigorously, waiting.

Luis said, "It's true, we have the Fordson. Still, is this enough? Milk machines should be installed and we need another tractor, a heavier one, complete with all the attachments; and after that, a baler. Why not do our own baling?"

"And you're willing to do all the work?" the old man said.

He was very diplomatic. "You'll have to teach me, Tio."

"Have you any idea how much?" the old man asked.

"About ten thousand . . ."

"I won't do it!" Madruga had said. "Why, I've run this place all by myself up to now. In my old way. No gadgets. My hands and back. I leveled this ranch, me, a team of mules and a Fresno scraper."

"The way I see it, the entire place should be plowed, scraped again."

"You've been doing a lot of listening, *rapaz*. They do a lot of talking at Corvello's, don't they? They talk about me, I know, call me a miser. And suppose I agree to do what you say, spend my savings?" The old man said no more and went outside.

Luis wrote on finally: *I hope this will find you both well as I am at present, thanks to God.* And again he paused, thinking of his father and mother out there, lonely, praying for him.

Suddenly he recalled a more recent, painful kind of absence. Concha had left Pamplona. The police had asked her to leave, and according to de Castro, she must never ever come back. "Good thing I cut the mayor's hair regularly, otherwise . . . These fellows can't understand we have to have a woman around to care for the needs of our people, working like horses, and away from everything . . . two dollars isn't too much to pay for some kind of relief."

The enclosed check for two hundred and fifty dollars will bring much happiness to our money lender. Please pay him in full, and the balance, not too much as you can see, use it for something you may need; perhaps Mother will buy a piece of wool goods for herself, and you, Father, a pair of shoes for Sunday, and if there is any money left after that, buy some sugar, coffee and a meat roast.

Again he paused, leaning back on the chair, feeling the cool breeze on his neck. After a moment he continued: *Tio Madruga treats me as if I was his son; still, I must work as hard as anyone in order to earn fifty dollars a month and board. But I don't complain because I'm young and the ranch is one of the finest around. One day I feel I may be able to lease a part of it, have my own dairy, buy a car, and save some money besides— you can do all this if you work hard in America.*

It was strange. He was running out of things to write about. A few months before, when the images were vivid and the ache in his heart hadn't yet given place to a strange, dull feeling, he could have written pages and pages to his parents. Now, with the passing of the months, he was beginning to forget. *I haven't much more to say, dear Father and Mother. Please pray for me, and tell our priest I am well, and doing the best I can in this big land. P.S. Tio Tomé sends his regards.*

"Better register your letter," Madruga said, "a good precaution." Smiling, "When your folks see this draft, you'll become famous. Your name will be in everyone's mouth."

"I guess so, Tio."

"Seeing you writing away makes me wish I had someone to write to. D'you know, I haven't received any letters from anyone for years except a couple from your parents before you came, and bills, of course." Luis waited. "But enough of this nonsense. What I want to say is I've made up my mind finally. I mean, I'll buy the equipment you mentioned the other day, and the plumbers will be here tomorrow to install the milking machines. How do you feel now?"

The boy got up and put his arm around Madruga. "Tio," he said, "Tio."

"Wait," the old man continued, "the real surprise is next. I'm going to clean, repair and paint our house and buy a new refrigerator and a new stove. But one thing, our old wood stove must stay. I want good healthy heat to make us feel fine in the winter and besides we have so much cottonwood around the place . . ." Luis nodded. "And there will be a better table set, new furniture in every room, carpets . . ."

"Oh, Tio!"

35

"And that is not all. I've decided to employ a new milker, a married man whose wife will do our cooking."

Luis remained silent. "You are the cause of all these changes, of course. Your steady ways, I mean. Your youth, your willingness to stay with an old man. I'm very happy."

"Thank you, Tio."

"Don't thank me, for all I know when I tell you . . ."

"Yes. A new milker means more cows. A new string."

"That's what I bought yesterday. Thirty fine three-year-olds. They'll be yours in about ten years. Naturally, you'll have to pay for them."

"How, Tio?"

"You have a strong body, haven't you? That's what counts in America."

Luis nodded. "How much?" he asked.

"Six thousand." Smiling, "Why, ten years is nothing. Then I'll give you a bill of sale and a lease on half of the ranch. Sixty acres and a barn. What d'you say?"

"Don't you think ten years—I know I haven't a cent but . . ."

"D'you know a better way?" Madruga asked. "A safe, fair way for both of us?"

Luis seemed to be thinking it out. "Yes, Tio. Why can't I buy the cows outright? Pay the rent first, then whatever there is left, after expenses, I mean: a few dollars for a pair of shoes now and then, and a few other things I can't do without, and rent half of the ranch. What d'you say to that?"

"You forgot one thing, boy. Interest. It's the blood of business in America. Without it Mr. Romano would have to close his bank." Luis waited. "Let's see, 5 per cent should be a fair return on a loan."

"Yes, Tio."

"Well, then, we'll go to Pamplona tomorrow and write it out."

The old man kept his word. In the morning he drove to Corvello's and asked the old man to contact his friends in Oakland or Sacramento by phone. He needed a milker and a cook; a married couple could take care of the matter. He'd pay well. Yes, he would tell the applicants the house was like new, newly painted and furnished; a middle-aged man would be just fine, Madruga explained to his friend.

"You want me to do this for you," Corvello asked. "Are you ready?

Doesn't everybody know you live in an old, dilapidated place? Painted, did you say? Furnished, eh?"

Madruga caught his friend's rambling thoughts short. "All I say is true. Or will be. The painters and the carpenters are starting tomorrow. I'll go personally to the furniture store."

"I can't believe it," Corvello kept on repeating. "You, the stingiest man in Pamplona!"

"I just want a little life around the place before I take permanent residence in that certain olive grove on Center Avenue. A boy full of dreams, a woman cooking our meals." After a pause he said, "D'you know I feel like fifty today?"

And as Madruga was about to leave, "Wait, wait a minute." Corvello turned around and opened a shelf from which he took a bottle and two glasses. "Here, let's have a drop. We must celebrate your rejuvenation."

"My what?" Madruga wanted to know.

"The finding of your youth. And let's hope it will stay with you a long while."

They drank the sweet wine slowly without a further word.

Next morning the first contingent of workers arrived at the ranch. The carpenters arrived first and began the addition to the house. In a way, it was a mere partition of the front porch. The bathroom would have to be there. Then the plumbers arrived and the electricians. The painters came last, and finally the place began to look quite lovely—white, green-trimmed. Luis and Madruga had been everywhere during the process, helping the workers whenever their help was needed.

The old man had forgotten nothing: the tankhouse had been painted; the broken glass panes replaced; linoleum put on the floor. "As long as you insist on sleeping here," the old man explained, "you might as well have a decent place. You are, after all, the cause of this change."

What the old man was doing was, of course, the cause of much talk in Pamplona. Some people said quite openly that he was crazy. Why spend so much money, he was too old to enjoy anything, a man without a wife, and it was too late to start getting silly and . . .

Still, others said he could find a wife right now; all he had to do was shave, put on decent clothes and smile; and with his money, he didn't have to smile at all.

And besides, who could tell how long he'd live? These old-timers were strong as horses. Everyone knows whalers live a long time; it was the salty sea and the food they ate, like medicine, some of it was.

The old man did not concern himself too much about the gossip. In fact, he enjoyed it and said so. Meanwhile, a man from Brown's Furniture drove over with a truck full for delivery. There were beds, mattresses, a good rocker, soft to sit on; not to mention all that was needed in the kitchen, all white, the latest thing. And a radio, too, and Madruga heard again Portuguese spoken by various radio "directors" beaming their programs to the Luso-Americans of California. Now the house was well-furnished, perhaps a little out of place for a dairyman's residence, according to some of the neighbors.

But there was no ill will towards Madruga. He had long been a part of the community, could always be counted on for the gift of a fat cow for the annual Pentecost Feast. Frugal he had been up to now, it was true. But if he wanted to change, they did not blame Luis for bringing it about. Here was a boy from the Old Country, less than six months in America, a diligent boy who had cleaned the ranch yard, and burned the weeds, planted vegetables in a plot—why that boy merited everyone's admiration.

Mr. Silveira was Pamplona's only notary capable of speaking and reading English and Portuguese. He did willingly many things for his clients: wrote their letters, executed powers of attorney, prepared their tax returns. His office was never too neat; he had the habit of saving everything, forms of all description, any printed matter. Sometimes he had a little difficulty in finding this or that document, but a patient search usually uncovered what was missing, much to the relief of everyone.

"Oh, it's you, Mr. Madruga. Come in, Luis." He closed Plato's *Republic*, using as a marker a tax form, and waited.

"We're going in business, the boy and I," Madruga lost no time in coming to the point. "I'm turning over to him a string of cows: six thousand dollars, five per cent interest. He can't sell without my say so; you know how to write these things." Turning to Luis, "You want to say something?"

"I will keep twenty-five dollars for my own expenses, and pay what is left to Tio until he is paid in full—something like that."

Mr. Silveira wrote down what was said, and he said to Luis, "You're very lucky, *rapaz*. Less than a year in America and already in business."

"He's not *that* lucky," the old man said. "D'you call it lucky, working like a horse every day of the year?" And smiling to himself, "Well, I want to make a real man of this boy; show him how to be somebody; and let me tell you, you can't do it by reading books or moving from place to place, never too long anywhere."

"When will you have the papers ready, Mr. Silveira?"

"Come in tomorrow," the notary said.

"We'll be here," the old man said and turned to Luis. "Let's go home, partner." He put his arm about the boy. "Black on white," he explained, "that's how we do things in America."

Mr. Corvello was responsible for the oncoming house warming. For one thing, he wanted it to take place on the evening the new cook and her husband would arrive. Luis and Mr. Madruga, he felt, should not be called upon to clean the kitchen—a woman must do it. May as well get used to the old man's household.

To arrange the party had been a simple matter. The women of the colony were anxious to see the old man's house and new furniture, and what had been asked of them was simple indeed. Some brought a loaf of sweet bread, a pie, or potato salad. Tio Corvello would himself furnish the crabs, clams and a twenty-pound fresh tuna, now in season, which he himself would marinate and bake.

On Thursday Mr. Corvello was told by telephone that a couple had been found willing to come and work for Madruga. "Only two days away," Corvello had said to a milker friend. "Do me a favor, go and pass the word around, tell the ladies to be ready." Then he called Monterey: "At least two dozen crabs, big ones, well cooked, plenty of salt. Clams? The littlenecks, yes. Half bushel will do. Be sure everything is fresh, you understand?"

It was eight in the evening when they drove into Madruga's yard. The women got out first, talking and laughing, carrying the food. The men followed, stopping momentarily to look at the yard. "I must say it, it doesn't take too much," Mr. dos Santos said, "a bucket of paint, and somebody willing to scrub and keep a place clean."

"How true, José," Frederico Leal said.

"Anyway, this is now the best set of farm buildings around Pamplona."

"And the best land. Let's not forget it grows everything. Not a spot of alkali anywhere."

"Yes," Isaías Ferreira agreed. Then, "We better go up and eat some of our food."

"And drink my wine," Gabriel said. "Hope it's good. I won it at a raffle the other day."

They walked in and felt a little lost and embarrassed. Such luxury! A carpet in the living room, imagine! And a sofa, not to mention the chairs, leather and cloth-covered, all no doubt very expensive. They finally made their way to the kitchen, feeling that they'd be safe there. But the kitchen was also something wonderful to see. Why, any woman would be quite happy to cook and be here all day.

Madruga seemed to be everywhere, while his new partner had been assigned to entertain the women in the living room.

"You take care of the ladies, *rapaz*," the old man had said. Shy as he was, Luis did his best.

"Why did I have boys instead of girls?" Mrs. Ferreira said. "Here's a young one already in business! What a husband he would make for some lucky girl!"

"I don't want to get married, Tia," Luis said laughing, "not yet."

"And why?"

"I've got obligations to discharge. I can't afford a woman; besides, I've just arrived."

"Oh, it's true," Mrs. Leal said. "It's true. Still, it's hard to live alone, especially when one is young, and it's natural to look for a girl, even a light-headed, married one, willing to taste the devil's fruit." Mrs. Leal waited, remembering, "Of course, there is always the chance of some trouble after that, as all of us well know. But thank God, Pamplona is now clean as far as our colony is concerned. What I mean is, married men stay married and young boys marry. A wife is the sure cure for a man's fever."

"Which reminds me," Mrs. dos Santos said, "when is this cook and her husband coming? Am I to understand . . ."

"This evening, Tia," Luis said. "Tio Corvello said they'd be here."

"And where is he?" Mrs. Ferreira asked.

"He's cooking the *petisco*," Gabriel explained.

"Oh," Mrs. Ferreira said. "In the Old Country during those days when the sea was asleep like a kitten, we used to walk to the seashore and get our fill of limpets and squid. I can still taste the sea in my mouth."

"And it's silly to feel this way. We have everything here: bread and meat, all the good things. We work for what we have, but it's always here, and a lot of it, thank God."

"Maybe so, but the taste . . ." Mrs. dos Santos was quite emphatic about the matter. "Don't tell me our apples and oranges weren't sweeter."

"You just think so, *filha*," Mrs. Leal said. "The trouble is we have our bellies full. We know no scarcity and naturally . . ."

A knock on the front door gave Luis the opportunity he wanted. He left the room to be greeted by Tio Corvello. "Come and help me, boy. I brought along a little food."

"Why, Tio?" Luis asked. "So much trouble."

"It's not every day we come over to wish an old friend good luck in a new venture in which you, too, are a participant. What I mean is, we're just Portuguese feeling good and getting together."

Luis followed the old man to the car and brought the food into the house.

"One thing about this *petisco*," Corvello explained, "I cooked everything, the fish, that is; I want no leftovers. It's got to be eaten, all of it."

"Too bad our kids prefer the movies to being along with their folks," Mrs. Ferreira said. "Comes the evening and you got to let them go. Otherwise, they threaten to leave and go to the city."

Mrs. Leal nodded judiciously, saying nothing. Now there was food everywhere: on the sink, the stove, and the Frigidaire. Mrs. Leal and Mrs. dos Santos were in charge of the table, meanwhile admiring the tablecloth and silverware. "Whoever furnished this place," Mrs. Leal said, "didn't forget a thing . . ."

"How true," Mrs. dos Santos agreed.

The coffee was ready, chairs placed around the table. "Let's go in," Madruga said. "I can't understand it. Why this fuss about us?" He wiped his eyes with a large, red handkerchief.

"Never mind, Tio. You sit right here. This is your place. And you, Luis, on his right. That's it," Mrs. Leal said.

Corvello stood a moment, facing his friends. Lifting his glass, he said, "I'm not a speechmaker and if I say something now before we eat, it won't take long. I may have to go back, you see." He paused a moment, tasting the wine.

"Where did you get this, Gabriel?" But before receiving an answer he continued, "What I want to say is that we came to honor an old man and his protégé. We congratulate both and hope the young one will be wealthy and the older one live to see it. May God bless them. And now let's eat."

The crabs had been pre-cooked early in the day and put on ice. Tio Corvello hadn't forgotten a thing: all the legs had been cracked; it was easy to pick the white meat with one's fork. "And there's the clams," the old man said, explaining, "cooked in their own juices and salt water. Help yourselves."

Now silence was almost general around the table. Their smiles and smacking of lips told Corvello this was indeed something wonderful. They were almost too full to enjoy the tuna, which even Corvello was ready to admit was really something.

"I marinated it myself, the way my mother did, and I tell you, just the smell . . ."

Madruga had somehow saved his appetite for the tuna. He ate it, great mouthfuls of it, grunting his pleasure now and then. "In my whaling days, yes, the fish tasted like that."

"You'll be able to eat decently again, Tio," Mrs. Leal said. "A woman cook—where is she from, I wonder?"

"From the Azores, of course. She and her husband," Corvello said. "And they should be here. Let's see, the train arrives at ten and it's past that hour. Everything has been arranged, though. They'll go to the pool hall and ask to be brought here."

"All these dishes to be washed and put away! We really should do it, help the poor woman. I'm sure she will be tired from the trip." It was Mrs. Ferreira speaking.

"We'll do it, *mulher*."

The men left the kitchen and walked onto the porch. They sat on chairs and on the steps, taking in the cool air, still pleasant after the passing summer. Their conversation centered on current prices, on how to produce more milk without buying extra feed.

"It can't be done, Frederico. More milk means extra animals, and naturally feed. When you start buying it, there goes your profit."

"How about raising something besides alfalfa? Clover they say, will feed a lot more cows."

"That's what I intend to do," Luis said.

"This spring?" Mr. dos Santos asked.

"Milking machines will save us time. We'll have extra hours in which to do other things."

Madruga beamed, hearing Luis talking like this. "If it's *ladina* you want, you shall have it. The seed is expensive, but they say it lasts a long time."

Corvello was the first to see it. A car drove up Saint George's Road, slowing as it approached the gate. "I bet it's the milker," he said. "Luis, go to the car and get their bags, whatever they may have with them."

The driver, Mr. Lucas, greeted the boy. "I was on my way home from the pool hall and these two asked for the old man. They're staying with you, they said."

"Thank you, Mr. Lucas." He spoke to the newcomers. "My name is Luis Sarmento. Mr. Madruga is waiting for you."

"We should have been here an hour ago, but the train stopped here and there, all the way from Sacramento, every little town."

"She's no older than Concha," Luis thought. This was, to say the least, a perverse comparison; yet the Mexican girl had been the only woman he had known. But there was more that brought about the similarity. Her walk, for instance, was a little suggestive, without, Luis felt, her being conscious of it. And he wondered about her face. In the semi-darkness of the yard, he hadn't as yet seen it. As he entered the porch, he saw her lips, full, well-formed. The face without a blemish, and the eyes, dark, by turns restless and pensive.

"Your name?" Luis began lamely.

"Ana Linhares," she said. "And this is my husband, José."

Madruga shook hands with the newcomers. To Linhares, he said, "All I expect of you is to milk, clean the milkhouse, do some of the marketing, irrigate—a hundred-twenty acres, between us three, we should have no trouble. The cows, by the way, will be milked by machine."

"And my wages?" José Linhares had a thin voice, like a boy's. And he was fat, weighed at least two hundred pounds. His arms trembled with fat, as well as his belly.

"Didn't Corvello suggest . . ." the old man said carefully.

"A hundred a month, board and keep, but if my woman is to cook . . ."

"Of course she is," Madruga said. "That's why we are hiring you in the first place."

"Then you'll have to pay another fifty."

43

"Too much," Madruga said. "Why, I could hire two milkers."

Linhares did not answer. Turning to his wife, he said, "We better go back." He spoke to the group of silent men. "I suppose one of you could give us a ride to town?"

As Mrs. Linhares lifted the small bag, Luis said, "Wait, *senhora*." To Madruga he said, "We should reconsider, Tio. We can't take care of seventy cows and do all the other work besides. You, of course, will help, but the idea of an extra man was to make things a little easier for us. What I mean to say is this man and his wife"—he knew Ana's eyes were on his—"are worth a hundred and fifty a month; for my part, I'm willing to pay my share of the salary. Are you a good cook, *Senhora* Linhares?"

44

"I do the best I can," the woman said. Her voice was sweet, without bitterness. Then she added, "But we don't want charity. I think we'll be worth our salaries."

"Come in and eat something," Madruga addressed them. "A few of our neighbors came over to give us a housewarming. There's plenty of food."

The old man introduced the newcomers to the women. "This is José Linhares and our new cook. You both sit here. There's some crabmeat left and tuna, marinated and fried as we used to back in the islands."

Ana Linhares smiled.

The women asked the usual questions. Where was she from, what island, how long had she been in America. Only four months! Why, it's like yesterday, isn't it? Ana nodded.

"Doesn't it still hurt a little?" Mrs. dos Santos said, "When I first came, you know how it is, everything is new in this big land, the way they dress, the food, and then we don't do things we used to do back there. No Holy Feasts . . ."

"Easter, Holy Ghost and Christmas, that's enough if you want to become worth something," someone said.

Mrs. Ferreira waited until Mrs. Leal brought a stack of dishes to the sink, and whispered, "Why, she's only a girl and so pretty to be . . . He must be at least fifty. Could be her father."

"Things happen sometimes," Mrs. Leal said. "I suppose her husband went over there, did some tall talking, and she was willing to come; our girls will do anything to come to America. You know that."

Mrs. Ferreira nodded.

"And now here she is, so young, in this house, and Luis, so eager. And we must say he's handsome. We're due for a scandal, I feel it. Everything points to trouble: Madruga, an old man, and the girl's husband all blubber, and did you see her eyes?" Mrs. Leal crossed herself and began to wipe the dishes.

"I think it's time to go home," Corvello said. "I've got to close up my place for the night. Besides, these people get up early; three-thirty will be here in no time."

"Yes, we should go," the men agreed. "These people are tired. They want to sleep."

"We're glad you're going to be our neighbor," Mrs. Leal expressed the feelings of all present.

"Thank you," Ana Linhares said. "There's enough to last us two days at least." She was collecting the food and placing it in the Frigidaire.

"Unless you ladies want to take some with you . . ." Madruga said. "As you can see . . ."

After they had gone, Madruga addressed his new helpers. "You do the best you can, and that will be enough. Luis will show you what to do. Whatever he says; when in doubt I'm sure he'll consult me; after all, I'm the owner. You understand?"

"We do," José Linhares said.

"Well, then, better come to bed. I'll show you your room."

Linhares addressed his wife. "You better come, *mulher*."

"As soon as I finish with the kitchen."

And as Luis prepared to leave, Ana said, "Perhaps another cup of coffee? I could—it's a luxury I didn't have whenever I wanted it back there."

"How true," Luis agreed. "But I really have to go."

The young girl reconsidered. "Perhaps tomorrow? I want to thank you for what you did for us this evening." Smiling, "It was you who really gave us the job." Then sipping the coffee slowly, "The big city where we worked last month. . . . I don't like factories. The fresh air, away from everything—I imagine the ranch must be like that."

"It's lonely sometimes," Luis said, "but if you are busy, and get tired doing what you must, you don't feel so bad after a while."

Ana Linhares did not answer.

"Good night," Luis said. Mrs. Linhares followed him to the door and closed it.

CHAPTER 5

It was four o'clock and the new milker was still in his room. To Luis, already in the yard, this was most disturbing. Linhares should be ready at the appointed time. Tio Madruga had told him what to do, the time to get up, summer and winter. He recalled the old man's directions that first afternoon of his arrival at the ranch: in the hot months three in the morning; in the winter, four.

Finally, a light in the room told Luis the milker was getting up. Madruga, he knew, would join them later. Luis and Linhares would be in charge of the stripping, but only to a point. Madruga's plan was to let the two men alone, see how things would turn out. Then he'd decide.

The yard was wet from the first heavy rains the week before. The ground under the gravel bed gave way a little as he walked back and forth, waiting. The sky, partly cloudy, reflected the still unsettled weather. As far as he could tell, rain would return again to the valley. He could tell by the sharp, cold wind tingling his face.

Back home at this time he would still be in bed, warm, under heavy homemade wool blankets, listening to the sound of his mother's feet, so soft on the pine floor as she walked to the kitchen to cook breakfast.

And what a breakfast! Taro was sweet, warmed over hot coals; there would be a bit of salt fish perhaps, and coffee, black and very hot. What kind of breakfast would be served this morning, he wondered? Would Mrs. Linhares do miracles with food as did his mother?

"Good morning," the new milker said, walking down the steps into the yard.

"Good morning," Luis said. The reedy voice of this heavy, almost clumsy man startled him. Should he be scolded for being late? He decided to speak of the matter later. He must get acquainted with this man, know more about his habits. "We'll go and drive the cows into the barn," Luis said. "Let's see, you go up the ladder and fork some feed down to the mangers. The machines are ready. I had them set last night," he added as they walked toward the barn. "Ever done much milking before?"

"I've done everything," Linhares said. "I haven't been in America thirty years for nothing. Name some kind of work, any work, and I'm sure I can show how it's done." The man, Luis thought, spoke without bitterness, more with pride.

"Anyway," Luis explained, "in this ranch things are done *our* way, and even this may be news to you."

It was amazing to see Linhares climbing the ladder with easy-going agility. He forked the feed down to the mangers in an even way so that all the cows received an equal amount of hay. Luis nodded his approval, seeing this.

"Feed them; keep them happy, then milk them," Linhares said, his gold teeth showing in the dim light of the barn. "I've been around, you see . . . dairies—it's nothing. But I'll say, I don't like to milk. To me it's a job. You get paid and you eat food fit for pigs sometimes." There was a pause. "But it won't happen here. My woman will take care of us, if she gets what she needs to cook with."

"You'll get the stuff; no one has ever called us stingy, not to my knowledge."

"And a day off a week, do I get that? I like to play a hand of cards now and then. I won't stand being cooped up here seven days a week."

"We only milk on Sundays. No outside work."

"Not enough," Linhares said. "I mean a day off all day. Doing nothing."

"I'll have to speak to Madruga about this."

"I thought you were his partner?"

"I am, but the old man will have to approve this new idea of yours. Do you know he gave me my first chance in America?"

"I know all about it. To work like a horse a long, long time, then one day, if you're lucky, you'll get a piece of paper saying you're the owner of a few cows, maybe ready to go into something else, just as important."

Luis listened in silence.

"Then you'll get old before your time, maybe die of cancer or something and what's left after you kick the bucket will go to the county unless some smart *preta* comes along . . ."

The cows in the mangers were eating, lowing now and then. Small birds, startled from their slumber, chirped, up in the rafters.

"One thing about me, I won't be tempted by the offer of land and cows. I'll just earn a few dollars, work a month, maybe two months, then go to the city all by myself."

"And your wife?" This was a rather personal question.

"My Ana is a green one. Only four months in America. Let her stay here and cook. After all, she has to earn her own living."

"Let's milk," Luis said.

Could it be possible? Here was a woman just come to America, and beginning to be ignored by her husband? He wondered why she had married this man, so positive and brash in his behavior. Momentarily, he recalled Ana's appealing face, the tired resignation . . . almost fear.

The milking proceeded quite normally until Linhares came to Chamarrita. The animal seemed to shiver, as his large hands touched her udder. And then in a flash, it happened. The cow's hind leg kicked the half-filled bucket, spilling the white foaming milk on the cement floor. Then the cow's heavy body came in contact with Linhares, pushing him backwards, dangerously in the path of another. The milker got up at once and like a man possessed, began to hit the cow with his fists, again and again and, still mad with rage, he bit it on its neck, causing it to bellow with pain.

"*Filha da puta!*" Linhares said. "You wanted to kill me, didn't you! Well, I'll kill you myself."

It was then that Luis interfered. He placed his hand on Linhares' arm, pressing the soft flesh. "Don't do that again! She's a dumb animal and is nervous like some people. Chamarrita produces a lot of milk. Leave her to me. I'll finish stripping her."

"No devil of a cow is going to kill me! I'll use a pitchfork!"

"You won't!" Luis said. "I'd rather pay you a full day's wages and ..."

Linhares, calm now, went on stripping his string to the end without incident. When they had finished, Luis said, "I should have told you about her. It's really my fault."

Linhares nodded. "There's animals like that in every dairy."

It was then that Madruga walked in the barn. To Luis' surprise he

49

had shaved and wore his Sunday clothes. "I'm taking the stage to the city at nine. Thought I'd go down and see the places where I used to spend a lot of time when I was young."

"Good idea, Tio."

"And how did the work go this morning?"

"Fine," Luis said. Then after a moment, "José is a good milker. We'll do fine together."

"Let's go in and eat a bite," the old man said.

They walked to the wash trough, which on Madruga's order had remained as it was: old and ample, where a man may douse his face and hair at will without the limitations of modern plumbing.

As the two milkers walked in the kitchen, followed by the old man, they found breakfast ready. And what a breakfast! There was sweet bread toasted, left from the evening before, and eggs, bacon, all fried just so. And very hot coffee.

"I don't know, boy," Madruga said. "This kind of breakfast will make bums out of all of us. This is so good, *senhora*! I would have been too, had I had the good sense to hire someone . . . The point is my partner, even though he didn't say a word, wanted to know the food of America, and it took you, *senhora*, a Portuguese, to introduce it to him."

Ana Linhares sat beside her husband, eating finally. "It's wonderful to have something to cook with," she said. "Back home we had to depend on the good and bad years to eat; and there was never too much."

"You're in America now," Madruga said. "And I hope here in this house . . ." The old man waited. "I needn't tell you I like you already and, I hope, Luis, too."

"I'll do the best I can, *senhor*," Ana said. "Cooking, working in a factory, or a fruit orchard, it's all the same." Then, after a pause, "But I like it here. It's so new, everything smells so good . . ."

"You talk too much, *mulher*," Linhares said. "Go on! Bring me some more coffee."

Ana got up and refilled his cup. "More eggs and bacon? There's some potatoes left . . ."

"I'll take them," Linhares said. And to Luis, ". . . unless?"

"Eat, man," Madruga said. "We don't mind feeding our working people." And to Mrs. Linhares, "You tell Luis what you need to plan a meal, say a day or so ahead. We'll get what you want."

"Why don't you call the store?" Linhares said. "Haven't you a telephone?"

"Not yet . . . I made an application for one. One of these days . . ."

"Which reminds me: whenever you want to go some place, tell us. The truck will be ready." It was Luis talking. He was proud of a driver's license, his first, just received from Sacramento.

Linhares said, "As long as Mr. Madruga is going to the city, I'll drive him to Pamplona. Besides, I need a hair cut."

"Good idea," Madruga said. And to Luis, "D'you think the Willow Field is too wet to plow? Maybe we should sow barley, what d'you think?"

"It'll assure us a little green feed for our cows." Then, "And the other land? *Ladina*?"

51

"If you like." And getting up, "We better be going, José. You don't mind if I call you by your Christian name?"

Linhares shook his head. "I'll go in the room and get my hat."

"Yes." And to Luis, "Now that you're in charge, do as I would have done myself. Your best, I mean."

Luis followed the two and walked outside. The winter sun appeared through the clouds. The wind had died out. In a little the sky would clear up.

Oh, it was good to be out here, all by himself, so much to do, and spring not too far. And now that the house wasn't empty anymore—a woman coming to the place had changed all that, the usual chores wouldn't be so hard to do. A good thing, for Pamplona was an empty little town since Concha's departure. "Like I said, boy, I like to have someone up here to accommodate my friends; but so far, nothing. Oh, one shows up, now and then, but only for a day or so. The police come and, tell the truth, I don't mind. No girl is worth fifteen dollars, and that's what these little *putas* from 'Tia Juana' ask; so when the word gets out, the Chief comes in and it's either leave or go to jail. They usually leave, thank goodness."

His only memory of a woman then had been Concha, an immigrant girl who remembered her town and liked to talk about it.

Returning, he saw Ana weeding the ground around the rosebush near the steps. And again that persistent thought came back: why, she was a mere girl! How old . . . he wondered how old she was.

"This is my job," Luis said, approaching. "And it's true, I should have taken care of the roses sooner, pruned them."

Mrs. Linhares stood up facing Luis, and again he noticed her eyes, large and very black. Her hair, abundant and of a chestnut color, was gathered tightly away from her forehead. It was quite long, and it shone in the sunlight. She wore a simple dress and as she washed her hands in the trough nearby he saw her long and slim fingers. "The kitchen is clean. I've made the beds, and I thought I'd walk around the yard. You don't mind, do you?"

"You do what you like," Luis said, "and if you need help . . ."

Ana thought a moment. "I will ask you to do something for me, then, a silly thing, really." Luis waited. "I'd like you to build a window box for me. Something to fit outside the kitchen window, and . . ."

52

Luis nodded. "To fill with dirt and plant a few *manjericos*."

"How did you guess it? Their smell will recall my home in the Azores. They say they are the herbs of the poor."

"You at least wish for something," Ana said. "You know what you want and go after it." Then, "Did José tell you when he is coming back?"

"He's getting a haircut. And then a game of cards, and another and another. But he'll be back for the afternoon milking."

"I hope so. Sooner than that."

"Oh, you don't know my husband. And I'm just learning to know him myself. We've only been married seven months, you see."

"A new bride!" Luis said, smiling. "Congratulations."

"Thank you, still I don't see why you should—unless it's because I'm in America as the result of my marriage. For this, I am glad."

"What happened, Ana?" Luis asked. "Do you care to tell me?"

They were facing each other near the newly white-painted stairway. The girl waited a moment.

"There is still some coffee left from this morning. I don't know why, but I'd like to tell you. Let us go up. It's not an exciting story, I must say."

They sat at the table facing the open window. The sunlight, warm for December, entered the room. It was so quiet everywhere: the ranches around them appeared; small groups of buildings of various shapes, gray and red, scattered here and there in the paling fields, show-ing the effect of the first frost.

"If only the sea was outside . . ." Ana paused a moment to sip her coffee. "This house reminds me of our home back there. We could see the entire village from it. Oh, I was happy enough, but that sea spoke of many things—America, mostly. And then I met José Linhares, a Portuguese who had become an American."

"Old enough to be . . ." Luis stopped talking. It was improper to talk about a woman's husband away from his presence.

"My father?" Ana said without anger. "Everyone said that in the village. He's too old, they said; still, I wanted to leave, like any young boy and girl." Smiling, "Didn't you?"

Luis nodded, watching her.

"And, as you know, the young ones, those who leave our misery, don't ever return to stay. Here they find a better life, marry—sometimes the old ones go back for a short visit, and you know what happened to me."

"Yes."

"When José came you should have seen all of us bidding for his attention. Why he selected me, I don't know."

"Oh, he was quite a *prosa*; proud as a peacock, new jeans every Sunday; a stout man with the voice of a child."

"Is he good to you?" Luis said, and then again, "But who am I to ask?"

"It's all right . . . anything you want to know. I must talk . . ." Luis waited.

"Our wedding, by the way, was something very special. Linhares hired a band, ordered good wine, a fat cow was slaughtered, the entire village invited, even the head of the municipality. We danced in the Pentecost Hall until after midnight; two weeks later I left my parents and came to America. And how strange it was! As soon as I left, I began to know the real José Linhares. It didn't take long to know." Luis waited.

"Fisherman, fruit picker, sheepherder, milker—he had done everything, been everywhere. But now he says he will stay in one place long enough to earn a few dollars, maybe do what you've done. He should have started long ago."

"But surely he had some money. He visited the Azores, a big wedding, and of course, the passage fares. I've just paid mine. The way you go about things, I don't know you too well, not yet; still, I'm certain you'll succeed in America. But José—who knows?"

"You're lonely, Ana, and you must fight your confusion by doing what you must do. Make of your husband your own project. Change him if you can. Make him do useful things. You are his responsibility; he must be made to understand that."

53

"He treats me as if I were a child, not a woman. Why did he marry me? I'll tell you. He is proud; he wanted to own something very special. But when I said yes to his question of marriage, he didn't know that it was America I was giving myself to . . ."

"And now?"

"I am already being punished for my deceit. Married to José, I have had no time to know this land, what it really is. Since I've been in California, I've already been in three places, a few weeks here, a month there . . . My father used to speak of the life on the ranches where one could grow enough to feed his family, a place where your children grew up and you grew old." Ana's voice became suddenly tender.

"You're lonely, Ana," Luis repeated. "It will pass."

"I don't want to travel all over and see nothing."

"Stay here as long as you wish. Consider this your home."

"I want to. Oh, I want to."

"What's important is Madruga's approval of your man's work. Should I say something to José, perhaps a word of advice?"

Ana shook her head. "No, Luis. I will, myself."

"You do that. And now I better get to the ditch fence. The wire needs tightening."

"You'll be back for lunch?" she asked.

"Yes," Luis said, getting up. "And make it light. We're not used to a big midday meal. In the evening, yes."

Two days later Madruga returned from the city. "Can you imagine? In a week, next Thursday, to be exact, it will be Christmas! You should see the people buying presents in San Francisco. Thousands! And the stores! All decorated like altars on Feast days back home! Oh, there were so many things to buy!"

They were eating supper, which these days was always a pleasant experience. This evening Ana had cooked a fine fish stew, thick with potatoes and seasoned with herbs and hot peppers.

"A good fish stew always brings tears to my eyes," the old man commented. "Thank you, girl."

"I was thinking of home this afternoon," Ana explained, "the way my mother used to cook for us, and there was this dry *cavala*, and I thought I'd fix it for our supper." Smiling, "But you must have had some wonderful things to eat while you were in the city."

"O yes, *filha*. But you know us Portuguese: we'll eat anything that swims, three times a day."

"I'm Portuguese myself, but I like steak and roast beef. Thank God, I've been in many places where you can have it at any time," José said.

The old man was hurt by this remark. "Haven't we been feeding you as we should, José? Ana, perhaps you've been failing your husband. Is it steak he wants?" And to Luis, "You must see about this, boy."

"You buy what you think is needed, Tio," Ana said. "My husband will eat what I cook. We are working people, and as long as there is enough …" Ana's voice trembled as she said this. An uneasy pause ensued.

"Anyway, what is important is that Christmas is approaching, and this is your first away from home, Luis."

"And mine, Tio," Ana said.

"Come to think of it, this too will be my first real Christmas in America. I mean, when I was young, in those far off days, I didn't have the time. I was alone then. Cooking my own meals, always in a hurry. There was a lot to do and I wanted to do it."

"And, I suppose you almost killed yourself trying," Linhares said.

Madruga smiled. "Well, I did work and thought of the future a little, instead of complaining about the food. And I saved a few dollars, yes. You have to when you have certain obligations to meet." After a pause, "And now tell me, you've been in California a long time, thirty years, is that it?" But José did not answer. "And in that time, what have you done? Any other Portuguese would . . ."

The falsetto voice was even more noticeable. "I may have no money, no cows, no ranch, sometimes only a few dollars to live on; but I can tell you this: I've seen California. I've been everywhere, and there's nothing I can't do, nothing."

"José," Ana Linhares said, "don't be foolish. Don't talk ourselves out of a job. This is a good ranch. Let us stay this time."

"Which reminds me," Madruga said, "instead of arguing as typical Portuguese, let's go out. I want to take a look at our cows. Haven't seen them in two days and I miss them."

Linhares followed Luis and the old man while Ana remained, trying in vain to hold back her tears.

Tio Corvello explained the matter to Luis. "Christmas in America? Well, the people buy a few presents; I myself sell a lot of extra cigars, boxes of them, and maybe a bottle of Port, things like that. But what counts is the idea behind it. Why, a kid will be happy to receive a bar of candy so long as we say Merry Christmas!" Then after a moment, "So you want to have a little celebration at the ranch this year, is that it?"

Luis smiled, listening.

"First of all, you go to the grocery store and buy a tree. A little pine tree, not too big, and then you buy a few pretty things that glitter, decorations, they call them. Then you go home, place the tree someplace and the woman of the house does the decorating. Of course, you too can help." Luis nodded.

Corvello was enjoying the young man's curiosity. "And then the presents. You place these under the tree, and I suppose there should be a little something for everybody." There was a pause and the old man asked, "Anything else, you'd like to know, *rapaz*?"

Luis shook his head. "I'll go to the store now."

"Like I said, don't buy too much. Remember, an orange or a slice of sweet bread was enough for us in the Old Country."

Outside now Luis heard de Castro's voice. "Hold on, boy, hold on. May I have a word?"

"What is it, *senhor*?"

"Good news, I think. If everything goes well, I'll have somebody upstairs next week. From Mexico City, knows all the tricks, is even better than Concha, I'm told, and you've got to admit that girl was pretty good. Charges a little more, three dollars, I understand. But the boys who have been to see her in 'Tia Juana' say she's worth ten."

"Thank you, Tio."

"I'll let you know when she comes. A little favor, between us—after all, we're Portuguese."

"Yes, Tio," and then, "Merry Christmas," he said in English.

"Oh yes, that's right. Merry Christmas."

"How strange it was," Luis thought, walking away. Soon he'd be given the chance of knowing another woman and already that mounting excitement troubled him, and he had tried to get used to the loneliness of the ranch. But when night came, that photograph on the calendar became Concha, and dreaming, he felt her fingers caressing him.

Later, he would wake up, feeling embarrassed and disgusted as his own hands touched the sticky and wet reality of his dream.

In the morning he promised himself to work harder, to drive himself on and on; those ideas of sin from his catechism days suddenly attained terrible importance. He must never again . . . yet, when he least expected, and nearly always in the comfort of his bed, the old fires returned. They came without warning, and the very silence of the place, the bright lights of Pamplona, even Ana's helplessness seemed to feed that throbbing awareness, that desire for release. And the coming Feast of the Nativity was not in itself enough to bury the forming image of that girl which de Castro would soon have in his place . . .

They placed the tree in the living room and decorated it. Luis had followed Corvello's advice and bought the decorations in the five-and-dime store. The little colored light set pleased the old man. He sat there watching the lights, the tree and the few packages under it.

57

"Tell me, boy, who told you how to do all this?"

"All you've got to do, Tio, is walk up and down Main Street and watch the stores. But I talked to Tio Corvello and he told me what to do."

"That old man," Madruga said, "what will we do when he's gone? Where will we go? Thank God we have a pool hall proprietor and a notary of our race to advise us. We'd be lost without them."

"Don't be a fool," Linhares suddenly said from a corner where he had been silently looking at the pictures of a magazine Luis had purchased. "No one is so damn good that you won't be able to go on when he dies. If you know the language of this country, and I do, you can go anywhere. You don't have to be where your people live. You go anywhere. All you've got to be is a citizen, and that I am. I may not have anything, but I can vote for or against the President of the United States."

Ana did not seem to hear her husband. "We used to fix the crèche in our parish church, my mother and a few of our neighbors. We gathered rocks in wicker baskets and they were so light; they said they were chunks of lava from a volcano long dead. We placed them on the altar, just so, and in no time the *presépio* was ready. Very strong, too."

"It's so strange," Madruga said, "here I've been away half a century. Think of it. And still I remember how everything was then; and you are right, Ana, we used rocks, not trees."

"In America, Mrs. Leal said this morning, the Feast of Christmas is for the children."

"I don't know about that, Ana," Madruga said. "I think it should be for everyone. And I should have felt this way long ago. Why go to Corvello's to eat his beans? Yet this I did, year after year. Not this year, though. We'll have our dinner cooked right here. What will we have, Ana?"

"Mrs. Ferreira is roasting a big turkey. They raised it, she said, and …"

"We'll have a turkey ourselves. I'll go to the butcher and select the tenderest. And more than that, for one thing, we'll have some taro."

"I'm going to bed," Linhares said suddenly. "You people can talk about food all night for all I care. I've got to be up at four."

"Good night, José," Madruga said.

"And don't you stay up late," Linhares addressed his wife.

There was an uneasy silence in the room. "What's the matter with your man tonight?" Luis asked.

Ana shrugged her shoulders. "It's the way he is," she said. Then, "May I have a little white angel? Yes, that one."

As Luis handed it to her, her fingers touched his and remained thus for a moment. Luis felt her warm, soft flesh, and he thought he saw tears.

The tree was decorated finally. Ana and Luis knelt before it in silence. "It's beautiful," Ana said. "If only my mother were here to see it."

The old man got up finally and, as usual, walked on the porch to watch the sky and guess the weather to come. Luis, too, walked towards the door and prepared to leave. "Good night, Ana," he said. There was an uncontrollable tenderness in his voice as he said this.

They drove—Ana, Luis and Tio Madruga—to Midnight Mass. As expected, Linhares preferred to stay home, for his own unexplained reasons. It was a cold and clear night. The entire countryside was silent as they drove on; the tall weeds glistened, frost-covered on the road banks.

Driving, Luis almost wished the road would go on forever. He felt Ana's nearness, smelling so good of the violet perfume he had just given her as a present. He recalled her husband's comment. "The smart ones give nothing and try to get a lot. Me, I don't believe in presents. But if anyone gives me something I say thank you and that's that." And then he had gone to his room.

They were now walking toward the church entrance, and when Madruga moved away from them to talk with friends, "José should have come with us tonight. It was his duty, really." After a moment, "But he doesn't love me. He married me to show the village that he could. He may as well be dead, Luis. Do you know, he has never . . . " Ana lowered her eyes, became silent.

"I've never felt so good," Madruga said as they reached the yard later. "Do you know, this is the first time—one forgets about these things in America." After a moment, "That's why I kind of understand Linhares. For all I know, this time of change isn't here yet. Perhaps in a few years . . ."

"I don't think so, Tio. I know my husband too well."

"It's late," Luis said, "Good night, Tio." And to Ana, "I can't wait to taste a slice of your sweet bread tomorrow. Merry Christmas!"

Ana walked a step or two towards him as if she were to shake his hand. "Thank you for the perfume," she said.

Tio Madruga put his arm playfully around her, saying, "Come on upstairs, *rapariga*. Your husband is waiting . . ."

CHAPTER 6

It was February and again the rains had come to Pamplona. The new alfalfa recently planted would certainly benefit from it, grow fast, for the warmth of spring was already being felt everywhere.

"This will be a good year," the old man said. "Listen to it fall! This kind of rain is worth many dollars, every drop of it."

"How many inches have we had so far this season?" Luis asked.

"Five and a quarter, that's what they were saying at Corvello's yesterday. Before the season is over we may have a total of seven inches, a normal amount."

"I see."

"More rain, less irrigation. We won't have to pay for extra water. That's where some of the profits go."

Luis nodded.

"Water and repairs. We should do our own, if we can, by taking things apart, knowing what to order. It takes time to learn, but when you know what to look for . . ."

"Yes, Tio."

"Repair bills can break us in no time, *rapaz*. That's the trouble with some of our dairymen. It's always easier to order a thing done while we play a game of cards at Corvello's. Don't ever do that," Madruga warned, and then he said, "But I'm talking like a fool. Ever since you've been here, you've taken care of everything and done a good job of it, too." He scratched his beard thoughtfully. "And what pleases me more, you are making money. Can you imagine, you've already paid over eight hundred dollars on your contract! I'm really proud of you." The old man went on, "After the rain we'll work the north field and plant *ladina*. We should have done this before, but as you know, the land leveler did not get to us when he should."

"It's not too late, Tio."

"By the way, where are Ana and José?"

Luis shook his head. "In their room, I suppose."

The old man waited. "Tell me, boy, are you happy with José as a milker?"

"Why do you ask?"

"Because I think he is not the kind of worker I wanted. The way he talks, such a sharp tongue! The only thing that saves him from getting the boot is Ana. She's a good cook, isn't she?"

"Yes, Tio."

"First you, and now this girl. You two have brought life to this house. I can't imagine how I lived here alone all these years."

Luis waited, listening.

"Isn't it too bad, a girl like that, young and pretty, married to the crankiest milker I ever saw? I say it again: it's her ways that save her man."

"We've got to learn how to live with José. Myself, I just let him talk."

"Is he kind to our animals, boy?"

"I guess so," Luis lied. "Oh, at first, during his first milking, he wanted to hit Chamarrita. But I spoke to him about the proper way of handling a string of cows. He grumbled then, but I think he understands now."

"I hope so. That's one thing I won't tolerate here: cruelty to our animals."

They saw Ana returning to the kitchen. "See what I mean," Madruga said. "There she is, always concerned about us. Why, we could brew our own coffee, we're doing nothing. Still, she won't let us do a thing."

After supper that evening they heard it. "It's Mansinha, Tio," Luis said. "She's about to calf. She's in the horse barn."

"Good. One of us should be with her. Animals are like people. They need your company."

"I've made a straw bed for her near the mangers. If you don't mind, I better go to the barn now."

"Wait for your coffee."

"I'll drink it later, Tio."

It was good to be inside the musty building. A single electric globe gave dim reality to the walls and many objects stored inside. There were old harness lines and a saddle hanging near the entrance; and in a corner, a surrey, borrowed every year by the committee in charge of the Pamplona Springtime Festival.

Luis sat on a mound of dry hay, waiting. Now and then Mansinha moaned with pain, contracting her body convulsively. Whenever this happened, he got up and patted the sweating animal. "Soon now," he'd say. "Why, your calf will be here in no time." This was silly talk, he knew. Mansinha got up and began to moan very loud, her forefront hoofs pawing the ground while a great expelling movement continued, more often now. There was intense urgency on the part of the animal to deliver this live being, who by its own movements denoted its own eagerness to come out into the world. Luis became fascinated, watching. First came the water bag, then the head of the calf . . . The birth was over in a few minutes. The black and white calf now stood on rubbery legs beside his mother.

63

Luis saw Ana enter the barn and walk to where he was kneeling beside the calf. "I didn't know how long you'd be, so I brought some coffee."

"Thank you, Ana," Luis said. Then, "Is it still raining?"

"Yes."

Now the calf had found his mother's teats and began to suck. "Watch him," Luis said, "just born and already he knows what he must do. It's the instinct to live."

"Lucky for him he is with his mother and will be for a while."

"It's different here," Luis said. "Bull calves are sold after a few days, little heifers placed in a corral and fed, away from their mothers. This treat," he pointed to the calf sucking away, "won't last long. In a few days a buyer will drive in the yard, make us an offer, and if agreeable, take it away."

"Drink your coffee," Ana urged. "It's cold outside; I sweetened it already, a spoonful of sugar twice, is that right?"

Luis nodded. "Is your husband sick? He is in bed, isn't he?"

"Yes."

There was a long silence. Luis asked. "What's the matter between you and José?"

They were both watching the calf as he tugged at his mother's udder, the little tail swishing back and forth, denoting his pleasure and excitement.

"My husband wants to leave the ranch. Tomorrow, next week, in a month . . . he won't stay here and be a slave to the old man. 'No more cows,' he says. Fishing, yes. Fished in the old country when he was young. And in New Bedford." Smiling, "This time it will be San Diego. He knows some people from the Azores down there. He'll go after tuna, go to far places, south. 'Pamplona is too small,' he says. Never again will he come back to the San Joaquin Valley. I am against leaving and said so, and for the first time he threatened me. 'You're my wife,' he said, 'You'll come with me wherever I go.'"

"And . . ."

"You should have seen it. When I answered, José walked toward me, forced me to sit and listen to him. His words trembled. I expected to be hit. Instead, he sat on the bed, buried his head in his hands and kept saying, 'I've got to go away. This is a prison.' There was anger and pity in his voice as he spoke."

"Naturally, the proper thing to do is to follow."

"I'm not going," Ana said. "I'm not going to wander all over California, knowing no one. It takes time to know people. In Tio Madruga I found a man who likes me as if I were his daughter. And I love this kitchen and all the fine things here."

It was his own understanding that made him do it. He took her hand in his, saying, "José is your husband, Ana. You must obey him. It's up to you to try and change his plan. Yes and stay." He waited, then cautiously he said, "But perhaps we failed you."

Her hand pressed his firmly. "No, Luis." Then she said almost in a whisper, "In a way I wish you had."

In the dim light of the barn her face appeared so beautiful. He was fascinated by the large eyes filled with tears. Now she covered her eyes with her hands, the fingers moving surreptitiously to them to rub off the tears, in a state of helplessness. Sobbing she said, "Oh, why have I come to America! Why have I met you, Luis?"

Then he was sure; it was a sin and he knew it—one of those unplanned meetings, flowering into friendship and then love, helpless and tragic. And he had in no way advanced its development. It was that living alone and coming suddenly in contact with a lovely girl aching as he was for those things recently left—a girl who spoke of outings in the country above her village, watching meanwhile the blue, endless sea. This girl so quiet, so diligent, had become against his will a participant in all of his dreams.

"Shouldn't we go back?" Luis said. "José may complain of our staying here together."

Ana was in a way prevented from answering. Without resisting, she lost herself in his embrace. "My dear love," Luis whispered.

And when he had kissed her, "Yes, I want to go back."

But Ana did not. Her body was sweet with tenderness. She wanted Luis and she knew he wanted her. All barriers seemed so easy to scale now. All matters suddenly were without importance. The element of sin, the scandal eventually to come, her husband's anger; she was ready for anything—a word, the compelling touch of his arms around her, his hungry mouth, how soft the mound of grass where they knelt.

"I must go back. We'll have another talk somewhere tomorrow." He held her hand as she backed away and kissed her departing fingers . . .

He watched for any sign of Linhares' behavior which might alert him to a knowledge of what had taken place in the barn the evening before. But the milker went about his work in his usual way; his bitterness continued. He was a fool to have come to this ranch; the ground was so wet, the corrals muddy holes. "Anyone operating a dairy to make a living should be examined by a mental doctor," he said.

Luis wanted to answer this oft-repeated tirade, yet he preferred to remain quiet this morning. In a little while he became convinced that Linhares was merely talking. He wasn't ready to leave the ranch—not yet. With the coming of spring and its pleasant weather, Linhares might become adjusted to his work.

As for Ana, she should not have come to the barn, and when she did, he should have told her to leave at once, but now that he knew how she felt, he would stay away from her, avoid being with her alone. He must if he could, even be rude to her. She was married, a mere cook, being paid for her work.

He thought, a good thing de Castro would soon have another girl, a very special one who charged three dollars for her love. And the work, he'd have no time to fall a victim to a lonely girl . . . Still, glancing at Linhares, dirty and unshaven, smelling of manure and sweat, so clumsy with fat . . . How could a girl, any girl, stand an animal like that?

They were stripping the same string, three or four animals between them. "This is our busy time, José. Our animals are calving. Dry stock and springers will soon be put out to pasture. There will be the first alfalfa crop to cut. But that will be easy. Machines do the hard work; we just sit on a tractor, or a baler. Thank God I've learned how to run those things and Tio Madruga . . ."

"You're his favorite pet, aren't you? Was I as young as you are with the same luck . . ."

"It's not too late, José. Fifty years, it's not too late in America. Look at Tio. Seventy and some, and he can do a day's work as well as any man."

"I tell you you've got to be young for this kind of slavery. It was all right a long way back. Then cows were cheap. You bought cows for twenty dollars a head, land for thirty dollars an acre. No wonder the old man's rich! He started out at the right time."

Luis waited, milking in silence.

"As long as I am supporting another mouth, the way I figure is to go to Los Angeles, San Diego, some big town, and find some easy job. I'd do it right now if I was single. I'd go to the old man, demand my time and beat it."

"Isn't Ana helping? Her wages and yours combined? Aren't jobs scarce where thousands live together? And besides, don't you like the peace of this place?"

"This is not the kind of California I want." After a pause, he said, "Because of my wife, I am here. It was she who thought we'd do just fine here, away from everybody. You see, they used to talk about ranches in her village, in every village, I suppose; of that *merda* of a country, and so my girl-wife—she's only a youngster, Luis, no experience, nothing—wanted to come here, begged me to come when Corvello called. So here I am against my will, but not for long."

Luis felt a shiver run through him. He thought of Madruga; what would the old man do upon knowing this secret desire of José's to leave?

And now he began to think of the monthly visit to Mr. Romano's bank in the morning. Tio had insisted on this: the monthly income would have to be figured out; milk checks; calves and old cows sold. Now, milking on, he thought of a way of increasing it—culling his animals, for instance. Come up on milk production by feeding concentrates. Oh, it hadn't taken too long to learn how to operate a dairy in the American way. Good feed and a lot of it—this would bring about that final payment on his contract ahead of time, years ahead of time. Then he'd lead a normal life, take a day off now and then, have a taste of women in a normal way. As long as de Castro would be around . . .

Linhares walked away to the milkhouse to empty the milk buckets.

"I can't understand it," Mr. Romano said. "Here's a boy who has paid his passage fare real fast and now is busy with a new obligation. Can you imagine, paid already a thousand on the contract! Better watch this Portuguese, man. Ask him to slow down, make him spend some of his money on other things like a new suit. Why, he doesn't have to dump every dollar . . . " The banker ruffled Luis' hair playfully. "You're really on the way, aren't you?"

"Yes, sir," Luis said in English. He was learning the language of America slowly. He associated with Portuguese exclusively, and no one of his acquaintances spoke English correctly; their words were a mixture of both languages.

Now and then Madruga would speak about it: "We were in a hurry to come here and went as far as the fourth grade, even less. Many of us only learned how to write a few words, sign our names and sometimes not too well. No one forced us to learn. All we thought about was America. Before California and its gold, it had been whaling. How could we do our hunting at sea and learn from the books?"

"It's wonderful," Mr. Romano said, "good to hear you speak English. Talk as best you can. Get a newspaper and listen to people, Americans, I mean."

"Yes," Luis said haltingly. "I'll do my best."

Leaving the bank, Madruga said, "I'm staying at Corvello's this afternoon. Go home whenever you want. I'll get a ride." After a pause he said, "Better still, have José come on down and pick me up."

"I'll get a haircut first, Tio."

"Take your time. The ground's too wet to do anything." He left Luis standing on the sidewalk.

There were several reasons why he liked to go into Mr. de Castro's barbershop. There was his fast-talking ways; the airiness of the rooms; comfortable chairs; and the pleasant smell of many lotions. And there were newspapers and magazines; and the little radio under the cabinet where the razors and combs were stored.

Sometimes three or four dairymen were waiting there; and it was then that politics or business, or even the latest scandal would be discussed amid laughter or thoughtful intensity. The subject under discussion this morning was Portuguese courage and how it sometimes manifested itself in what might be called a cowardly way.

Mr. de Castro was an expert in surprise endings, and seemed to be in good form this morning. All this came about when Mr. Lucas in a rather careless way, or so it seemed, said the Portuguese navy was the strongest in the world. He went a little further; if that big storm in the Channel had not taken place the Portuguese might have beaten the English . . .

"Wasn't it the Spanish Armada?" someone said. "The way I was told at school . . ."

"I suppose you're right," Mr. de Castro agreed. "And let me tell you, the Portuguese would have seen that storm coming their way and avoided it. I know nothing about the sea; still, I believe they would have been careful. We've always been." He stropped his razor listlessly, then continued, "This brings to mind Mr. Avila's sons, and how their father tested their courage."

"Avila? Does he live around here?" someone asked.

De Castro shook his head. "What I'm about to tell happened in the Old Country, long ago."

The barber shop was in complete silence now. "Yes, Mr. Avila wanted to teach bravery to his boys, and the safe way to accomplish it. So he told them what our priest would call a parable."

"Please go on . . ."

"The old man talked to the oldest son thus: 'Now think a minute, you're in enemy territory, the country is new to you, and nearby is a barn, ready to fall; in front of you is a manure pile. You're under gunfire so, as a brave soldier, you must do your duty. There is no officer to command you. You're on your own. Tell me, Francisco, what would you do?' Francisco was the eldest son."

"And this is what the boy said . . ." De Castro took a towel away from a customer's face. "'I'd run right back, father, as fast as my legs …'" De Castro paused a moment, then continued, "Now the old man turned to the other boy, Fernando, the middle one, and asked, 'And you, *rapaz*, what would you do?' 'I'd wrap the flag of our country about me, and with my gun blazing away . . .'"

Mr. de Castro's customer was now shaved and the barber dabbed a little powder on his face.

"And the third one," a dairyman began.

"Oh, he was the smartest one," Mr. de Castro said. "His father thought so, at least, when he asked David—that was the third boy's name—what he'd do, whether fight or run, and what do you think he said?"

Everyone waited in silence.

"I'd dive, face down, in that pile, father, deep in the manure."

"A young boy acting like that? What a shame!" Mr. Lucas felt very bad.

"To me, David was the bravest," Mr. de Castro explained. "The way I see it, to run back is cowardly; to march ahead and face certain death is a foolish thing; but to lie down and wait is the wisest act of all. You understand, don't you?"

"I think you're right," a customer said.

"Numbers, locations, time," de Castro concluded. "You've got to know what to do, a boy or a sea captain, in a sea storm or a manure pile."

The men in the room agreed, nodding their heads.

"And so we will leave the merits of our Portuguese navy and its strength to the men who write books. After all, this is a barbershop."

"And a place to do a lot of talking," Mr. Lucas said, getting up. "I've got to go back. It's about that time."

The others followed in short order. Luis' turn was next. "Please hurry, I've got to go back," he said. "Linhares wants to come to town."

"And you'll be milking alone?"

"I can manage—I've done it before."

"Too bad you've got to go," de Castro said. "She's here. Got in yesterday."

"I see."

"You ought to see her. Concha—why, Concha was nothing!" Smiling, "Go on up, now. Rosita is alone. Just knock and tell her I sent you."

It was the same approach, cold. You paid your dollars and that was that.

"No, Mr. de Castro, not today. I've got to go back."

"Like I said, as one countryman to another . . ."

"Thank you," Luis said.

He delivered Madruga's message, and for once Linhares accepted with pleasure.

"Go after the old man, stick around town, wait until he's ready? Good idea, I must say."

"When?"

"How should I know? Let Madruga enjoy himself for once. Five, six o'clock, what's a few hours? Do you mind?"

"Oh no."

They had met in the yard and Linhares called his wife, "*Mulher!*"

Ana answered at once from the kitchen window. "I won't be back for supper. Don't wait for me." And to Luis, "And thanks for doing my share of the milking, boy."

He had avoided meeting her alone, since that incident in the barn. And he wanted to talk to her, yes. He wanted her and in desperation wished Linhares would leave. Yet, if Ana followed her husband, would he be free?

The second test of his courage presented itself as he walked in the kitchen and sat at the table. Ana was excited a little, he could see, by the way the dishes were handled. There was a certain hurry in her movements, as if she were pressed for time.

"Almost two o'clock," Luis said for no reason at all.

A silence ensued and Ana began, "Oh, my husband must be very happy, playing cards at Corvello's. Who knows, he may even go to de Castro's rooms." After a pause, she continued, "Tell me, what do you know about that place? José has been telling me about the girls up there. He has been invited to go up."

"He's talking nonsense, Ana. Why, a married man wouldn't . . ."

"You don't know Linhares," Ana said. Then she said, after a long pause, "Do you know, I haven't been touched yet by him . . . but he demands awful things of me; I will not lower myself, married or not."

"Oh, Ana," Luis said simply.

"Let him go to those who will do as he likes."

"Should you call our priest and tell him?" This was a foolish suggestion, considering that a man past fifty would not change his ways or passion. It was too late to return to the innocence of the beginning.

"The priest!" Ana said startled. "No, Luis. We'll resolve our problems in our own way, my husband's, yours and mine." And then changing the conversation, "And now, we better eat a little lunch."

They sat facing each other. The cool air came in the kitchen through the open window. It was a delicious soup. To the kale soup Ana added a few potatoes and *linguiça*. It was seasoned with cumin seeds, garlic, onions and peppers.

"It's wonderful, Ana," Luis said, wiping his lips.

"I thought we might as well enjoy the food of our islands while we can." Then, "But I shouldn't talk like this. The new girl at de Castro's may be so good my husband will want to stay here forever."

"That girl at de Castro's, Ana," Luis began, "I, too, was invited to see her. Only this morning."

"You are free, Luis," Ana said.

"And I must confess I've been up there before. I couldn't help it. In my case I came out of that room as lonely as before. Two dollars worth of love? I want more than that."

"I myself want very little. Just a man to love and respect me. Someone I can nurse when sick, and work by his side when in good health. I want a home. Above all, I want a man . . ." Ana wiped her eyes furtively. "I'm sorry," she said.

It was then that he got up and went to her. He stood behind her and placed his hands on her shoulders. Then he kissed her gently on the neck. "You're upset," he said. "It will pass."

She did not move as she felt his hands closing over the round firmness of her breasts. That same sweetness she had felt in the barn had returned, dulling all scruples: the will to resist was gone. She let him lift her up and carry her to the bedroom at the end of the hall . . .

71

CHAPTER 7

In the yard finally he felt better. He had left her as soon as possible. . . .

This evening at supper Tio Madruga spoke of the special chore to be done in the morning. "You wait a year for this, boy. The winter months pass, the alfalfa begins to grow all over the place. Then, one day in April, even though this is done in the last week of March sometimes, you drive out and cut the first alfalfa crop of the year. It's a kind of ritual, you see. Thirty or forty years ago we did it with horses; no smell of gasoline then, just two healthy animals walking as you sat on a mower pulling the reins this way and that, and your horses seemed to know what to do." The old man smiled, remembering. "In those days there would be two or three men in the field cutting, and before long a kind of race began so as to know who would finish his portion first.

"It was like that in my whaling days, only the fields were the sea and the object of the chase a fast swimming whale. We just rowed and rowed and cussed and sweated. When I think of our island people in the Azores waiting day after day for a few whales to sound nearby, and how excited everyone got about it when it happened . . . the men running to the shore, the women and girls praying for brothers and sweethearts in those small boats leaving the shore . . ."

The old man paused a moment. "Indeed, our own race as to who would cut his share of the field first is really of no importance."

"All of us have to work, Tio," Luis said.

Madruga nodded. "Yet, when I think of those poor watchers out there and weeks go by, and not a big fish in sight . . . they need help, those poor Azoreans. No rain; sometimes the wind comes and then ..."

"All of us have troubles, even in America. I myself have been looking around for something better to do but with no luck, so far, and it isn't my fault," Linhares began.

Luis saw fit to change the subject at once. "And tomorrow, Tio, are we then to cut the first alfalfa of the year together?"

"Yes, boy. And do you know what? I'm going to do it with you. I'll drive Mr. Ferreira's Fordson. I can have it, he said, and you drive our own. How about that?"

"Let my husband do it, Tio," Ana said. "Not that you can't do it— why, anyone can see how excited you are already, but . . ."

Madruga smiled. "I don't know what being a father is, still I'd do anything to have you as my daughter, Ana Linhares. If I should lose you …"

José spoke finally. "You let me do it, Tio. Go to Corvello's and play a game of cards. Leave the ranch to us."

"Thank you, José, but there are certain things that only the owner of a ranch may do. Helping to cut the first alfalfa crop, for one." Smiling, "But it's true; I am not young any more. I mean, I should go to bed now and get a bit of sleep." Then he said to Luis, "And you, too, boy." And to Ana, "We'll be expecting a good breakfast at five. Shouldn't you . . ."

Linhares said suddenly, "I think I'll go down to Pamplona tonight for an hour or so." He got up and followed Luis outside. In the yard he said, "Why don't you come along, *moço*? Don't you like to sleep with a girl now and then? There's a new one at de Castro's. I understand she's good."

"See you in the morning," Luis said, walking up to his room.

He darkened the tankhouse and gradually he began to see things with a certain degree of clearness outside. The light in the kitchen cut a triangular bright figure on the yard, reaching away, almost touching the nose of the tankhouse.

Luis sat on the bed, still dressed, watching to see Ana's figure at the window. This, in itself, would be enough.

But it wasn't. When Ana appeared at the window later and stood before it a moment, he became all afire again. He walked outside, his feet crushing the gravel in the yard. He stood before the window and called softly, hoping in a way no one would hear. "Ana?"

After a moment the kitchen became dark. Was she offended? Had she heard his call and refused to listen? But no, Ana must come, adulterous as this action might be.

The door was opened and the girl walked down to where he was.

The moon was away from the sky, the darkness was general everywhere. Ah, it was better this way. His hands went knowingly to her, became lost in a loving caress. His fingers tingled with desire. "Come with me," he whispered.

"I'd better not."

"Up in my room. We can watch the town from there."

"I'm afraid, Luis."

"I am, too. Come, it will take only a moment."

And when it was over he talked soberly to her. "We mustn't do this again. In the beginning, I thought only once would be enough. But now we have to refuse each other. We can do it, I think." After a pause, caressing her still, he added, "I think we haven't tried to be away from each other. We give in too easily."

It was then the girl sat in bed, found his face and pressed hers against it. "At times, Luis, yes, I wanted to ask you to leave, the two of us, go somewhere . . . a new start. But we'd never be happy. Remorse would follow us like an invisible ghost and besides, you have a duty to make happy an old man's last years. You have your own future. I'm not worthy of all the days and nights you have spent here, denying yourself . . . and there is my husband and scandal that will follow us as soon as it is known."

"You must stay here," Luis said. "Do your work as if nothing ever happened between us. And if I ever again, I want you to tell José. He should at least have some pride in possession."

"Pride?" Ana's voice was angry and cynical. "Do you know every cent I earn, the entire fifty dollars, is kept by him, not only to repay my passage fare, but our wedding expense, too?" Luis waited in silence.

"As long as I refuse his animal way . . ."

Auto lights appeared on Saint George's road, approaching the ranch. "It might be José." They came together again, but only for a moment. "Good night," Luis said, adding, "Thank you." He watched her run inside, mounting the steps noiselessly. Then he moved to the spot in the bed where she had been and lay there quietly.

He was up at two thirty and walked to the cottonwood field to drive the cows back to the barn. It was so good, walking along the lane, step-

75

ping on tufts of wild clover, feeling its leaves wet with dew, brushing against his ankles. Birds sleeping inside the elderberry bushes along the way chirped in protest as he walked by.

Looking up, Luis attempted to guess the weather to come. But he had very little to go by. There were no clouds, no breeze, even the smallest constellation was visible. His animals saw him and without much coaching began to walk ahead of him, entering the lane, pausing now and then to taste the grass along the way.

As he approached the barn, he saw a light in the kitchen; Ana was up already preparing breakfast. And this was good; the way to do a real day's work was to start early. The old man had always done that. He must show Madruga that he would, himself, keep up the tradition.

But tradition or not, he felt a little uneasy on Madruga's insistence, that he himself drive the tractor again. His age was against a silly contest. Easy as it was, it needed concentration to drive in a straight line, avoiding possible holes and levees. Of course, he'd do it very slowly, making a great show of how hard it was, allowing the old man to win at any cost. He'd do this, and in the end he'd say, "You've made it, Tio."

Then they would laugh and they'd ride back to the yard, walk up to the kitchen and drink a pitcher full of milk. That was the way to do it, he had been told by Corvello, except that in the past the old man had won by fair means.

"Oh, he was a working fool, and of course, in the days of the horses it was better. Then you depended on their character and some of them, if you weren't careful, would run away with your rig; a barbed wire fence meant nothing."

In a way, it was tragic that the years were piling on the old man, and one day soon he'd have to quit active participation in the activities of the dairy. There must be a little more to life than banking twice a month or joining a few old-timers at Corvello's for a game of cards.

He found Madruga servicing the borrowed tractor driven in the yard the night before by Ferreira.

"You see, our neighbor takes good care of his equipment: greased and clean. Some of us leave it until it's needed. Naturally it costs a lot to put it in shape then. You mustn't be like that. If we took good care of our horses in the old days, why not these things?" Luis nodded.

"Should we go in and milk?"

"Yes," Luis agreed. "And where is José?"

"Asleep," Madruga said. "He'll be along at four-thirty, his usual time."

"He should be here now."

The machines sucked the milk into the sealed buckets with slow, quiet precision. Luis watched the old man walking along the string of cows. Now and then he paused by this or that animal and patted it, talking to it affectionately. "You're a great one, aren't you? Producing so much, and sometimes we cheat you a little bit when we should give you an extra forkful."

The smell of tobacco in the barn announced José's arrival. Without greeting anyone, he began stripping.

"It's about time," Luis said. "Or don't you know what day this is?"

"I know. The day before payday," José replied laughing.

"Anyone else would have been up an hour ago, gone to the field and brought the cows in."

"Listen, *moço*, I do what I'm supposed to do—no more. If you don't like it..." It was evident a state of hostility was developing between the two.

"Luis," Madruga said, "let's get on."

It was wonderful how the old man went about stripping; his hands, still firm and agile, performed the work unerringly; he was happy, singing, more like a hum than a song; it was a sailor's chanty, something about the sea when the great white sails crossed it in search of oil and that rare, always elusive ambergris . . . Luis suspected the old man was reliving his days as a whaler. He talked more and more of those voyages of wonder.

"I needn't tell you, José," the old man said, "you bring the milk to the creamery this morning."

Linhares grumbled his assent.

"We have no time for breakfast, have we, Luis? Look out there." The day had already begun. Now all that was needed was the sun. Way back where the old man had pointed, the sky was crimson above the small, irregular line of the mountains.

Their effort to avoid the morning meal was of no avail; Ana, possibly aware of their intention, was in the yard waiting. "Here's some coffee," she greeted them. "At least something hot, you really should eat."

"We have no time, *rapariga*. Besides, according to custom, we go out there on an empty stomach, do what we must, and then . . . "

77

"Drink your coffee, Tio," Ana said teasingly, her words sounding like an order.

The field waited at the end of the lane, and the two men drove slowly towards it, passing the barbed wire gate already open. Now Madruga and Luis were side by side.

"This is kind of silly," the old man said. "But do you know, it will be fun."

"Select your side, Tio," Luis said. "And remember, we have all day, and there's always tomorrow."

The old man nodded, driving away. The sun had finally appeared above the mountains, still without warmth. The tractor rose up and down a little as it drove over the levees—like the sea, the old man thought, driving on, green, fresh sea. Now and then a startled pheasant flew up to the sun, shrieking its protest. The race for the elusive whale of long ago and the race to finish the field this April morning meant one and the same thing: the earning of bread, much or little of it.

As he reviewed the past Madruga became excited by degrees. Harpoons and the driving wheels of a tractor—he remembered voices he had not heard in fifty years. . . . Should he signal Luis to drive on, faster and faster?

He called, "Hey, boy! Are you asleep?" Luis waved back, laughing.

The entire countryside was alive now with moving tractors. Mr. dos Santos was out there, and Mr. Leal, and farther away, Mr. Lucas.

Oh, Madruga felt so good, doing again a useful thing. And why not? Shouldn't a man refuse to accept advanced age, fight for his youth? A good diet was needed, naturally. Still, was there better food anywhere than milk? He had drunk it continually since his coming to California. No wonder Tio felt like a young man this morning. Except for one thing, perhaps.

For now his face was very hot and his breath came to him in little gasps. It was like a child's, short and fast. And now the sun was dancing all around him, and sometimes the mountains danced, a majestic, if erratic dance. "I'm a little dizzy," Madruga told himself. "I must take it easy."

He stopped the tractor and got off of it. Then he lay against it, his hands on the cab, his head resting against it. He was breathing hard; a sticky perspiration formed all over his face, a strange ringing sound bothered him. "What's the matter with me," he wondered. As he lay against the Fordson, a strange unknown fear came to him as if some impending tragedy was approaching. He was fearful of doing those normal acts he had always done, and which had seemed most natural to do up to this moment. Finally, after a few minutes, all things passed away from him, becoming like a fearful dream. The sweat on his face dried off; his heartbeat became slower. A hand on his shoulder brought Madruga to reality.

"What's the matter, Tio?"

"I don't know, boy. I should have drunk a little more of the coffee this morning. I should have had a little breakfast. You see, I suddenly became dizzy. I may as well tell you, I wasn't feeling too good a few minutes ago."

"You stay here. I'll go and get the truck. I'll take you to Dr. Barboza. You can stay in his hospital in case . . ."

"That little man? He doesn't like old people."

"You've never been to a doctor before. How can you say that?"

The old man nodded, still holding himself against the truck.

"I'll be right back, Tio."

"And the field?"

"I'll finish it tomorrow."

Dr. Barboza walked into the little green-painted waiting room to meet them. He was not too busy at this hour.

"Which one of you?" he asked. And seeing Madruga's pale face, "Don't tell me you've found the time to pay me a little call this morning—official, I can tell."

And when Luis told him what had happened, "Let's go in here."

Luis watched the old man sitting on a white stool, all the verbosity gone, still afraid.

"Take off your shirt," the doctor ordered. "And let's be as normal as we can."

"Doctor, I . . ."

"Are you trying to tell me you're in fine shape? You've never been to a doctor in your life? I know, you've been too busy making money and that's a shame. But someone told me you had retired. Didn't you?"

Meanwhile, Barboza was examining the old man. Luis noted his chest. It was lean, hairless, like that of a young boy.

"You've had a heart attack," the doctor said finally. "And it's a wonder you didn't die out there. Racing, did you say?" Then seated facing his patient, "Your racing days are over, my friend. If you want to live, and there is no reason why you shouldn't, you've got to quit working. Hard, exciting work, I mean. Direct your business if you want to, but even this must be done without worry. You've got this young boy coming up. I've heard all about you, Luis, how hard you are trying to be somebody. Let him be in full control from now on. Oh, you can do something—strip a cow or two, not too many, feed the calves; but the hard work is out." Dr. Barboza smiled: "You really have nothing to worry about. This one was a mere warning which you obeyed instinctively."

"Thank you," Madruga said. "And it's true. I really should have come to see you before; but you know how it is, one doesn't ever seem to have enough time."

"You call at Smith's on your way back. I'm phoning in a prescription." Then, "Luis, you watch him. Tell me if he misbehaves." And after a pause, "It's good to see somebody trying to get ahead in America." Like I said, don't let the old man make a fool of himself again."

"I won't, doctor," Madruga answered. "Now that I know what happened to me and what could have happened, yes, I feel better already." The old man followed Luis to the truck.

Madruga's heart attack should have been enough to make this a memorable day, according to Luis, yet more was to come. It happened during the evening's milking and Linhares caused it. It began when the milker, bitter and loud as usual, sat at the far end of the barn and began to strip his share of the cows. He did not feel sorry for the old man, not one bit, he said; after all, Madruga should stay home. He had enough money and land, what did he want? To take it all to the grave with him?

Luis did not say anything. The silence continued for some time, and then it was broken by loud curses. José had suddenly walked away from Mansinha, grabbed a shovel and hit her across her back. The animal stung with pain, lowed mournfully, trying to free herself from the manger.

"No goddamned cow is going to piss on my neck and get away it! I'll kill it!"

He was still holding the shovel as Luis approached.

"Don't come near," Linhares' falsetto voice was even higher, "or you'll get it, too!"

"Put it down," Luis said calmly.

Linhares placed the shovel against the wall. His hands were trembling. The red, sweaty face contorted. "Go ahead and hit me. I won't fight. I've made up my mind. I want my time! I tell you, no cow is going to do this to me, not again!" He continued, walking away, "At least, I won't have to get up at four every morning, not any more. I'm through with this kind of life."

"Listen," Luis had caught up to Linhares. "Do you realize it will take weeks, maybe a month, before we can find a new milker? Stay on for a few days, at least."

"I'm leaving tonight."

"Madruga is a sick man. And your wife—" Luis was almost careless as he said, "Ana likes the ranch."

"I don't care what she likes!"

They found the old man sitting by the window, watching Ana prepare supper. "What happened?" he said to the two men standing before him.

"I want my time. I'm quitting," Linhares said.

"He hit Mansinha," Luis began. "The animal dirtied his neck."

"Haven't you learned how to be careful?" Madruga laughed. "You who call yourself a milker! And besides, is there anything that water can't clean?"

"What I want to say is I'm quitting. Or don't you understand?"

"Don't you think the sensible thing to do would be to wait until I see Corvello and have him find another man to take your place?"

"I want my time. Now!" And to his wife he said, "Get your things together. We're leaving."

Ana, who had been silent, turned about from the sink and faced her husband. "I'm not going," she said.

"Oh?" Linhares answered. "And do you know this is the biggest news I've had since I married you? I'm free now. Free to do as I please, go anywhere. You weren't ever a wife to me, anyway."

"To submit myself to a pig! Is that your idea of a wife?"

Ana's face was flushed in anger. "You, who promised so much, now treat me as a slave."

"You refuse to be my wife. You're no good, Ana." And now his eyes on Luis, "Go ahead, *moço*. Try her. She's no good to me." He was unable to say more for Ana's slap silenced him.

"Go!" she said. "And stay away from me, *maricas*!" Then she rushed to Madruga and knelt at his feet. "Let me stay, Tio. I'll even work for less."

"Go and fix supper, *filha*," said the old man. And then, "But are you sure, perhaps this is only a quarrel. Tomorrow you may want to go."

"No, Tio. If I'm to be refused a place to live and work here, I'll leave, do anything, except stay with this baby of a man!"

Madruga waited an uneasy moment. "Go and get my checkbook, Luis," he said.

"Yes, Tio."

"A full month's wages. We'll pay him that." And to Linhares, "Do you want a ride to Pamplona?"

"I'll walk."

"How about supper? People don't leave this house hungry."

"It's all right."

Linhares pocketed the check, after examining it. Then without a further word he walked out the door.

"You know," Madruga said, taking his place at the table, "a day or so ago I'd probably get excited at what took place just now, but I remembered Dr. Barboza's advice and kept calm." He turned to Ana, "Time for my pill, ah, *rapariga*?"

She walked in the barn and sat on the milking stool just vacated by her husband and waited. "You may as well teach me," she said to Luis. "At home I used to milk our goat, stripping a cow is no different, is it?"

"You should go in," Luis said. "You're our cook and besides, you have another job now. Tio must be kept in the best of health." Then he showed her what to do. "It's easy, in a way. But I don't want you to learn. This is a man's job."

"Only until a new milker is found."

"Well, then, you'll wash the milkhouse and the utensils." He continued after a moment, "You'll need all your strength for other things. Your mental strength for one thing: for when the word of what happened reaches our neighbors . . ."

"Let them talk," Ana said. In the silence of the barn their hands clasped momentarily.

CHAPTER 8

Esteban Garcia's coming to Pamplona was a yearly event. Toward the
end of April or during the first weeks of May he arrived at Corvello's
place, carrying the usual sample cases.

"Put these under the counter," he'd say, "while I eat." And then loud
enough so that the card-playing gang at nearby tables could hear, "Do
you know I carry the finest assortment of samples and the least expensive this year? Never such bargains in my twenty-five years in business.
No Portuguese, no matter how fat and stingy, can refuse to buy a *roupa*
from me. Yes, on Holy Ghost Sunday the best dressed men will be
wearing my suits. Like these beans, what I carry is very special, and naturally, I can fit anybody—anybody!"

Garcia, a Spaniard by birth, spoke barbarous Portuguese which did
not in the least curtail his success in business. He sold suits wherever
Portuguese lived and worked, visiting early in the year the fishing
colonies in San Diego, then traveling slowly to Sacramento where he had
his home. He reached it during the latter part of July. Then he and his
wife would go up into the mountains for a two- or three-month vacation.

He sold suits under one religious pretext or another. There might be
a Cabrillo's Lodge convention, the Easter Feast, or Our Lady of Fatima.
Yet from a monetary standpoint the most important feast of all was that
of the Holy Ghost. For it was almost a rule that all Portuguese attend
the celebration dressed decently. The women, too, were aware of this:
they bought new dresses, shoes and hats at Penney's.

Garcia's system of approach was quite simple: after a night in town
he drove to the farthest ranch away from Pamplona; then came back
from there not missing a single ranch. A happy and talkative salesman,

he liked nothing better than to be asked to eat at some house along the way. Then he'd listen to the new gossip, exchanging his own in return. The sweet and stout variety of Portuguese home-made wine appealed to his taste. He usually drank two or three water glasses full of it, then slept.

It was generally agreed that Garcia sold more suits to the Portuguese all over California than anyone. Rare was the milker who refused his straightforward approach. And for those who had resisted, there was always another day, another celebration: Garcia always came back.

"Let's see," he greeted Madruga this morning. "I've been coming to your place since my start in business and every year you send me away empty-handed." Smiling, he continued, "Well, here I am again." He looked curiously in the living room, walking meanwhile into the kitchen.

"I can't believe it," he said. "Something has really happened to this place! What made you untie the money bags, old man?"

"Watch your manners, Esteban," the old man replied. "Walking into a man's house, sticking your nose in every corner—can't one buy a few gallons of paint, a piece or two of furniture?"

"Besides," Esteban said, "you have somebody here." And now with a bit of Don Quixote in his manner as he bowed, he said, "My lady, I am a poor suit salesman, and if I may be permitted to say it, you are truly beautiful."

"Beware of this man's line," Madruga said. "He talks very sweet, and it's a good thing he does not take orders for ladies' dresses." Then he continued after a moment, "Esteban, this is Ana Linhares, just arrived from the Azores."

"Oh," Garcia said. Then, carefully, "May I ask, is your husband's name José? I have just met a man, fifty or thereabouts, two days ago in San Luis Obispo. Said he had left Pamplona, left his wife too, and for good. He was going to San Diego to fish, that was the life, he said. He was very drunk, I must say."

"You saw my husband," Ana agreed.

"And he left a beautiful lady like you!" Garcia shook his head.

"Sit down and have some coffee," Madruga said. "And take your time, sip it, for I may have a surprise for you." Laughing, at the next table, he asked, "Tell me, how many calls have you made at this place?"

"Oh, I don't know, I have been at it for the past twenty-six years or so and I visited Pamplona on my first trip. I remember it well, for when I came the first time I sold every dairyman a suit—every one except you."

It was then Luis walked in and joined them. "And here is another addition," Madruga said. "Meet Luis Sarmento, my new partner. He, too, may need a suit."

"Indeed?" Garcia said. "A good one, grey, perhaps? No, blue serge for you. You're young."

"I have all the clothes I need."

Esteban smiled. "Next year, perhaps? Why not?" Now he turned his attention to the old man. "And you?"

Madruga startled him. "Show me your samples," he said. "Let's see what you can fix me up with. It will have to be a black serge. Of good material. After a pause, he continued. "The Holy Ghost's Feast, or one's funeral."

"I must agree," the salesman said, opening his sample case. "Still, the way you look to me, you're going to be around a few years. Quite a few."

And when he had taken the old man's measurements, he was quite careful about this. "A suit must always fit to perfection," he said. "Your *roupa* will be here in two weeks, no longer than that." To Ana he said, "I wouldn't worry about the loss of your man, *señora*. You ought to have seen him when I did. Filthy. You should pray never to see him again."

The confirmation of Ana's desertion by Linhares became a most important piece of gossip to Garcia. In no time the entire countryside knew about it. The women gathered in little groups after Mass and discussed it. The men talked about it whenever they met and, without exception, they took Ana's side. After all, an old bastard doing that to a girl who could safely be his daughter!

"It's a dirty shame," Mrs. Leal said, "Here's a girl in the flower of her youth. I can't imagine a man refusing a biscuit like that, I just can't."

"It's for the best, I guess," Mrs. Ferreira said. "Besides, the girl will find somebody. She should."

"Oh well," Mrs. Leal said, and there was malice in her tone, "Ana shouldn't have to go too far to find companionship. Not too far." She made the sign of the cross to ward off evil, insidious thoughts.

Meanwhile, José Linhares had not as yet been replaced at the ranch. Much to Madruga's amusement, Ana walked to the barn twice a day and did her share of the stripping. She did this enthusiastically and well.

85

Without saying so, Luis was proud of her adaptability to the dairy life. And, of course, it was wonderful to see her nearby wearing blue jeans and shirt of the same color, her luxuriant hair covered by one of his own caps.

"Now you better get out and go back to the kitchen. Do you want one of our cows to mistake you for José and kick you?"

"José who?" Ana answered in the same teasing way. "I don't know anyone by that name." But no matter how hard she tried to forget the ugly helplessness and the stupid pride, all those shameless demands which in themselves were the basis of Linhares' character, she could not succeed.

Now that Esteban had elected himself as courier of Linhares' desertion, the eyes of the colony were on her; her actions were subject to minute scrutiny.

Being near Luis, wanting him, aching with loneliness and desire, she remained outwardly calm even though the chance to love presented itself quite often. There were always the barns, the cottonwood trees by the canal, her own bedroom.

"I can't stand it any longer," Luis whispered to Ana one evening. "I've got to see you." There was no answer.

"Listen to me, Ana."

"I'm afraid, Luis. The way the women look at me, I can't help knowing their thoughts. It's that Old Country way of obeying your husband, no matter who he is, how old or what he likes. You must suffer, you can't rebel; this is your cross and you must carry it."

"Please, after supper? Just a talk."

"Just that, Luis."

He wanted to love her just now, carry her as she was to a mound of hay; or a grass field away from everything under the protection of the night, and there safe, the two of them lost in each other . . .

But they were not safe anymore. The specter of Linhares' absence kept them painfully asunder.

"You go to bed right after supper; we have to get up early tomorrow." Her smile was not mysterious. He knew she'd come.

Tio Madruga had bought every accessory at Ana's suggestion: a fine red tie, shirt, new socks and a pair of shoes. A new suit called for these things and, after all, one who was attending the Holy Ghost celebration a first time in many years should be properly dressed.

"How do I look?" the old man asked that morning.

He looked fine indeed, Luis thought, recalling the old whalers in his village back home. They, too, had gray beards covering their faces—not too long, just enough to accentuate the pink color in their cheeks. Captain Pimentel was one of them and Pereira and Trindade, that man of few words who lived alone in a stone house at the end of the promontory, just above the sea.

"Like a real *baleeiro*, Tio," Luis said. "Watch out, all the girls will turn around under one excuse or another to look you over."

"I have already one girl," the old man said, smiling. "All mine now since her stupid man left." His arm was placed fondly about Ana. "Yes, mine, Ana Linhares. You and Luis are all I have. Both of you have brought life to this house. That is why I ask, stay on, and all matters will come out all right. Luis, shouldn't we get ready to go to Mass?"

"I haven't a new suit, Tio," Luis said as though he meant it. "How can I go to church this morning?"

"Come now," the old man said. "If you didn't care to part with your money, it's all right with me. I suppose you know you'll have your indebtedness paid in half the time required. You're only a boy. Tell me, what do you plan after this?" Luis did not answer.

"Say it, *rapaz*."

"I'd like to buy the other half of the dairy, lease the entire ranch, Tio. Rent and payments—you'll have all the money you'll ever need."

Madruga smiled. "Suppose I have other ideas? Suppose . . . you know this is a holy day, money shouldn't be in our thoughts, should it?" He spoke with his arm about Luis.

Ana said, "I really should stay home, Tio. My name will be on everyone's tongue."

"You haven't done anything," Madruga said. "The way I see it, no man will defend your husband. One thing bothers me a little though—how will you free yourself from José? Forever, I mean? There are certain laws; I must go to Pamplona this week and see a lawyer. Let's go now. It's time."

It was like the Old Country, Madruga thought, standing by the church entrance watching the parade approaching. There were many flags, white, green and red, gold-embroidered; groups of men marching, representing the nearest Portuguese colonies: Monterey, Santa Clara, Tracy, Fresno and Sacramento.

These groups of marching men meant they were the whalers and gold miners who had come in the beginning, had stayed, raised families, bought land. There were others who had come after them and become a part of the New America. The old customs and traditions had been respected and passed on. The Feast of the Holy Ghost served as a means of grand contact for all, all over California.

The girl carrying the Crown was very pretty; she had a certain regal way about her. But then, every girl looked quite regal in the parade. It wasn't quite the same in his village back there, the old man thought. There a man carried the Crown and the people marched to the music of drums, cymbals and a Gypsy's tambourine.

After the Mass, a loud sermon in Portuguese, bands of marchers regrouped once more and returned to the society's hall.

"Should we join them?" Madruga asked.

"We'll drive, Tio," Luis said. "Barboza wouldn't approve of you walking ten blocks or so under the sun."

They arrived and waited until word was sent that the *sopa* was ready. There was food for all and as much as anyone could eat. Wonderful food, meat of many cuts cooked together, in large steel pots until tender, simmering in gravy, to which had been added twigs of mint and many spices.

"Oh, it tastes so good!" the people at the long tables passed judgment on the *sopa* this year.

"Well, a little more salt would have made it just so."

"And cabbage. It improves its taste."

"Someone should talk to the chef about this."

Madruga, Ana and Luis sat together and waited to be served. "Do you think Dr. Barboza would have any objection?" the old man began.

"No, Tio," Luis said. "I bet he has had his panful already, delivered early this morning." Smiling, he said, "As long as you don't overdo it."

"Now that I know you like it," Ana said, "I'll cook some whenever you crave it."

"Thank you, *filha*," said the old man.

It was then that Luis managed to hold Ana's hand under the table, saying, "Now look about you. Do you see anybody pointing our way, discussing us?"

Ana returned Luis' pressure. "Perhaps not, and it doesn't matter, really."

Outside the hall the old man was greeted by many old acquaintances. "It can't be Madruga! The *baleeiro*. How are you, Tomé?"

The old man sat on a bench, and now it was one and then another. "Can't believe it, here you are and I recall the time when you and Sarmento went whaling, to the islands of the Kanakas and Sidney, Australia. I left the sea about the same time Sarmento went home. Now you say this is his boy, and you are here, rich, I suppose."

"God has been good to me, yes. And you?"

"I own what I have always wanted, a pear orchard. Not too big— just enough to keep me in bread and milk the rest of my days. No meat now, you see, doctor's orders."

89

"Doctors have the habit of moving into our lives later in life, haven't they, António?"

"How true."

Now they all waited for the band to play. Men and women formed in little groups and talked, people from the many villages of the Azores visiting together in California.

Even José Linhares' name came into the conversation: Mrs. Costa and Mrs. Ferreira sat with Ana, talking to a few women visitors from Los Angeles. On being introduced, Mrs. Caetano said, "You must be the wife of that *trapaceiro*. Someone pointed you out to me and I want to say you should consider yourself lucky. We knew your husband. He worked for us for two months. My man fired him when he found him behind the barn doing things to himself, as if there weren't women around." Ana did not reply.

"Anyway, you're young and pretty. Why don't you come with us? We'll find you something." After a moment she continued, "But divorce that man. Do it, religion or no religion. Why, it would be a sin to go on being that brute's wife."

It was then that the auctioneer's voice was heard above the crowd, and the men began to move toward the corrals where the cattle offered in honor of the Third Person were about to be sold.

"Let's go and see what they have this year, Luis," Madruga said.

"We have enough cattle, haven't we, Tio?" Luis said. "Should we buy any more?"

The old man smiled. "It's true, I guess. Still, don't you think Ana should be given something? Isn't she a dairywoman now, since her man left? And doing good work besides?"

"Yes, Tio."

"What I mean is a few heifers, a secret between us. We'll fatten them up, sell them and give her the money as a bonus. After all, she is being paid as a cook, and this isn't too much." With his arm about Luis, he said, "Do you know I've never had so much fun in all my life? Meeting all these people, remembering old things and the food—the *sopa* was very good, wasn't it?"

The auctioneer sat on a fence and began the usual chant. There were many bidders and Madruga called it a day after he purchased five heifers, enriching the Holy Ghost Society by six hundred and twenty-five dollars. "I'd like to go home," he said finally, wiping the perspiration from his forehead. "Unless you two want to stay and dance awhile?"

"No, Tio," Ana said at once.

"Besides," Luis said, "it's nearly three. We start milking in twenty minutes."

On their way back the old man complained of being a little uncomfortable. "This *roupa*, and worse, this buttoned shirt." And teasing, "You insisted I buy all this, Ana; but truly, you didn't have to sell me the idea. I wanted to look my best. Did you notice everyone looking our way?"

Madruga laughed. "I think I'll take off the coat. Only a crazy Spaniard would think of selling a serge suit at this time of year!"

They were home finally and Tio said, "I'll set the table while you two get ready for the milking." Then, as if talking to himself, he said, "To think I wasted so many years living alone! Just to see old friends today, to know where they live in California; in what business, orchards, owners of grocery stores, all of them paying taxes, some of them citizens of the United States; yes, and their children, those who will take over later, going to college; learning their parents' business." There was a note of sorrow on Madruga's face as he finished, "Only on this phase I have failed; I'm just an old man who made a lot of money and has no one to leave it to."

"Why don't you relax, Tio?" Luis said. "Yes, a little sleep."

"And be sure and take your pill in ten minutes," Ana said.

"I will, *filha*."

The cows were lined up in the barn, the milking machines ready. It was then that Luis approached Ana and pulled her gently to him. "Oh, my darling."

But Ana remained passive. "What's the matter? What have I done?" he asked.

She said as if she had not heard, "When is the new milker coming?"

Luis shrugged his shoulders. "He should be here now. No later than this week, anyway. A fine man, Corvello says: wife and children in the Old Country. He will stay in America a few years, save something, then go back." Ana did not reply.

"Come, tell me what's the matter. Are you tired? Perhaps you should go in. I told you, this is no job for women."

"Oh, it isn't the work."

"What is it, then?"

Ana hesitated a long time. "I think I'm going to have a child, Luis. Yes, I am sure of it."

The sound of the animals chewing their food became very loud at this moment. "It's all my fault, Luis."

"You have done nothing, nothing at all. Instead . . . But this is no time for discussions. Later. How long have you known, Ana?"

"Two weeks or so. At first I wasn't sure."

"I see." Then after a moment, "What's important is that we go on, the two of us, as always. First, for your sake, and Tio's."

It was strange, but Ana's announcement had somehow cooled his ardor. Slowly he took his place at the string of waiting animals. A cold sweat covered his face. His mind now was an aching void as he went from cow to cow.

When he came to Mansinha, he suddenly recalled Linhares and his anger towards this poor, defenseless animal. He realized suddenly that the memory of this man would plague his days and nights from now on. That falsetto voice, yes; the bitterness and the pride; the worst of all, the fear of his return.

CHAPTER 9

From his room he saw Pamplona as he had every night just before he went to sleep. He recalled its houses, business places, churches and melon sheds, colorless during the day and neon glowing as now, noisy with music, a place where one could find solace or satiation—a card table, a bar, a pew or a brothel.

It had been in Pamplona that he had been initiated in what, if continued, could lead to tragedy. Now he was the father-to-be of a child, conceived in adultery and surely, insofar as the Portuguese colony was concerned, an unwanted child of sin. Ah, he should have listened to his father's warning—there were women in California sweet of tongue and easy of laughter, inviting in their ways. And to think he had disregarded his counsel! It was his fault; no one should be blamed for what had happened.

"But this is no time to dream," Luis told himself, undressing. There would be cows to milk in the morning, feeding and marketing. He'd be getting a supply of water to irrigate the ranch at noon.

And again he thought of Ana. "We must be truthful with ourselves, and inform Tio. When? How?" He could not answer these questions—not yet.

"The new milker is here," Tio Corvello called. The telephone had finally been installed in the Madruga household. "He just got in, and is eating a bite. Come by and pick him up whenever you want."

"Good. I'll have Luis drive down in half an hour."

"You'll be lucky this time. He is a well-mannered man, quiet, and his hands like hams!"

"Good."

"No *baboseiro*; I can tell."

"I hope not," Madruga put the receiver down and said, pointing to it, "Do you know this is a wonderful thing? The time it saves you. You call the grocer, the doctor, anybody."

"My husband was a great believer in it," Ana said. "I don't know when he got the habit or where, still he used it continually for anything, whenever he could."

"I wonder where he is?" Luis said. Then he became silent. Did it really matter where he was? Not for the present, anyway. Yet, as the days and weeks passed his presence in Pamplona would be tragic. San Diego? He had heard José say he'd like to go there and, no doubt, he had, or was already at sea for all he knew.

"I'll go and get the new man and be back in a few minutes." Luis got up and left.

"I really should go with him, find out how much the man wants, and so forth. I guess we can discuss that later. See how calm I am, Ana? The old days of bargaining are gone, as far as I am concerned."

"How do you feel, Tio?" Ana asked. She sat opposite him with her hands crossed in her lap.

"As always," the old man said, "except for one thing: sometimes I'm very tired. It's as if every part of my body is asleep. I sometimes count up to fifty, very slow, mind you, without breathing and nothing seems to happen. I don't do this too often, I'm afraid."

"You should be."

"It's not the idea of dying," Madruga continued. "Still, I'd like to be around a few more years. Why, you two young people in this house, it's something wonderful, seeing you two go about your duties; the noise of the young—do you know I used to run away from people such as you? How the understanding came about, how I changed. No, better not talk about it."

"The truth is, I may have to leave one of these days," Ana said.

"Leave!" Then, "But perhaps duty calls you to your husband." The old man's face was beginning to reflect his worry and disappointment.

"No, Tio. Not to José."

"Well, then," said the old man, laughter again in his eyes. "What is there to worry about? But I know: I'm not paying you enough. How miserly I have been! Tomorrow, yes. Tomorrow we'll have a new understanding—you'll get what they call a raise in America."

"I'm earning enough, Tio."

"Like I said, I want you to stay here. This is your place, don't you understand?"

"Yes."

"Which reminds me, is the new milker's room ready?"

"Yes, Tio." Ana suddenly laughed. "I hope he won't snore too loud."

"A little noise won't bother me too much, *rapariga*. Not since my sailing days."

Now they were quiet. Ana poured a little hot milk and coffee in Madruga's cup, filling her own. Then they sipped it slowly, wordlessly, for at this moment of full understanding, words were unnecessary.

"This is so good," the old man whispered and closed his eyes as if in sleep.

Mateus Aguiar, the new milker, proved to be what Corvello had guessed. He was not afraid of working and this pleased the old man a great deal. On his second day he went to the field and drove the cows back, all by himself. "I'll strip them all," he told Luis. "They're not too many." He did not seem to be doing too much at any time. His ways were slow but steady.

"Now, where has this man been?" Madruga said one evening. "Here we've been suffering, paying our money, taking insults from a man who respected nobody. Which reminds me, I think I'll go to Pamplona tomorrow morning. I've got to see the notary."

"Mr. Silveira?" Luis asked.

"Who else? He's as good as a lawyer, and charges less."

No one said anything. "We'll talk about your case, Ana. This matter of the desertion: what you can do, now that you don't know where Linhares is . . ."

"Perhaps I should go with you, Tio," Ana offered.

"No, not yet. What we'll do is discuss the matter. Just that."

The front door was opened quietly and Mr. Aguiar walked in. He sat down at the table and at once Ana filled his plate. "Fava beans, Tio. I hope you'll like them."

"Oh, yes, *menina*." After a spoonful, "They taste as good as my wife's. Her way of cooking, why she could take a stone, wash it, add a

few things to it, and in no time you'd have a most wonderful meal."
Then, after a moment he added, "Your mother, I'm sure must be an
artist. You've learned how to please a man's stomach and this is good."

"Thank you."

"I think I'll go to bed a little earlier this evening," Madruga said.

"I'll follow you in a minute," Mr. Aguiar said. "That's one good thing
I appreciate in America—after a good day's work, a good night's rest."

"He's a lucky one," Ana said after the milker was gone. "He'll sleep
without worries, think of his animals, the chores he must do, no more."
After a pause she said, "Do you know I hardly sleep these days? Only a
few snatches in the morning. I should be happy, for inside of me I have
a living baby. I want to talk to someone, open my heart, but I can't.
Whenever I see Tio, I want to cry. I want to tell him of our love and if
I do, he'd be quite correct in ordering me to leave. Then, what would
happen to you?"

Luis shrugged his shoulders. "I'd go, myself. We wouldn't be happy,
naturally."

Ana said, "We will eventually have to take Tio Madruga into our
confidence."

"It is awful to think of, yet we could say the child is José's."

"No. No, Luis. Let our sin be known by all. Nothing that we could
do, nothing will absolve us of it. Weeping won't, nor work. Oh I should
really hurt myself, do some heavy lifting. Perhaps in this way—but that
is a mortal sin, of course."

"You're upset," Luis said. "Please remember, whatever happens we'll
be together. In the end we'll find some kind of solution." He added,
"We need a little more time. Then we'll see Tio together."

"We must do it soon," Ana said.

"Let us walk a while, Ana. It's a cool night. Come."

A full moon shone above the countryside, giving it a pale, soft color.
Under it, the town seemed less bright; the neon signs merely indicated
it in the distance. Thousands of insects sang their summer song in a
great chorus, each group unmindful of the other, whirring and chirp-
ing together.

"Let us go to the far end of the ranch," Luis suggested. "Do you
think you can do it," he asked solicitously.

"Of course."

Luis smiled, his arm around her. "I was thinking of our child. Nothing must happen to you, or to him. Do you know, this a fine land, the finest? It would be a shame to leave it."

There was a pause as he continued, "Tell me, are you ever bothered by thoughts of your husband? Of his return unannounced, finding you pregnant? Would he speak aloud, or in pride keep silent and leave?"

"He won't return," Ana said.

He felt her arm around him, the fingers caressing his flesh. They had reached the end of the ranch. The field had been cut in the afternoon. The grass was soft and ample covering it. "Let us sit a while," Luis said.

"Oh my darling." In the abandon of the moment their worries were forgotten. There was a great hunger in their love. They wanted the world to fall away from them, to die as their love reached the great climax brought back with release, the same helplessness and confusion.

After a while, Ana said, "We should go back."

To the east of them a shooting star scratched the sky and fell gradually downward and in a moment was gone. "Oh, there are so many, many up there," Ana said pointing.

"You mustn't do it," Luis cautioned. "Or have you forgotten?"

"Bad luck, eh?" Ana asked. He preferred not to answer.

"What's the matter, *rapaz?*" Madruga asked him a few days later. They were in the barn alone. "What I mean is, are you worried? The old fever, I mean, is gone. Oh, you do the work and all that; still, you don't get excited about it the way you used to. There is something? What is it?"

The boy shrugged his shoulders. "I don't know what I've done, Tio. I milk, irrigate, feed our animals. What more should I do?"

"Your eyes speak of a secret worry, boy." The old man waited, noticing meanwhile the baled hay neatly stacked, touching the ceiling. "Whatever you've done, if you've done anything, I'm ready to listen. We ought to discuss things openly." He smiled. "I've lived a long time and maybe whatever has happened to you could have or has happened to me."

"Tio," Luis said, and hesitated. He was about ready to confess his guilt. But now Madruga seemed to have lost interest in what Luis was about to say.

"What is important is that you do have a problem. We will discuss it at the proper time, later."

"Thank you."

"Well now," said the old man, "I feel a lot better, knowing you have full confidence in me."

"How could it be otherwise, Tio?"

"Enough. Go and see if Aguiar is done and is ready for supper."

But Luis did not go, not at once. Oh, he felt sure now, Madruga must have guessed it for some time. Why had he questioned him, led him to a near confession and then abandoned the idea? Perhaps he wanted his own admission freely? His and Ana's?

He walked into the kitchen where he found supper waiting. But he refused to eat.

"I'm not hungry," he said. "I'll have a good breakfast in the morning." Then, after a few uneasy moments, he walked to his room.

CHAPTER 10

Mr. Silveira sat at his desk, the door opened wide, reading a Portuguese newspaper. The town was still quiet at this hour. He saw Mr. Romano walking down the street. Tio Corvello swept the sidewalk in front of his place; three Southern Pacific brakemen approached the pool hall. The good, pungent smell of melons ready to ship to eastern markets reached him.

At times like this, when the peace of the morning touched everywhere, Mr. Silveira did not regret his decision to leave his island home and come to America. It is true, he could have been somebody over there, a teacher or lawyer, no less. But he refused. America, that was the land his father had visited, a land so large it would take months to walk across it. Naturally, when one is young, how can one refuse the temptations unseen across the sea? So he had come to find the loneliness of the foreigner; to learn slowly, to work hard when his heart yearned for those things which only exist in the imagination of poets and dreamers.

In a way it had not been so bad. While he worked he had learned English methodically with great care and then one day opened an office, his own. PEDRO SILVEIRA, NOTARY PUBLIC, the printed letters on his window said.

They used to say around Pamplona that it would indeed be a sad day if Mr. Silveira should die, or leave town. Who would be able to take care of those who had never been able to speak English, who had somehow remained untouched by America?

This morning he did not have to wait too long for his first client. He recognized Madruga's truck a block or so away. "A good thing you're still alone," the old man greeted him. "I've got to speak to you, privately."

"I don't see why you had to bother me at this hour," Mr. Silveira replied. "Secrets, have you? Don't you think I could lock the door, the two of us inside, any time of the day?"

The old man nodded. "For one thing, you think better in the morning, my father used to say; and who cares to sleep when the air is cool, and there isn't a cloud? Look above you, Pedro!"

Mr. Silveira did and sighed. "How I'd like to be up in the mountains, at this time! Ever been up there watching the sun touch the treetops, smelling the blue pines, a forest of them all around you? You eat and eat, away from those things we call business in America. But it's silly to talk about that, just now. Tell me, Tomé, what troubles you this morning?"

"I don't quite know, Pedro. It's not money or land. I have enough of both, thank God. But what to do with it when . . . The natural thing to expect is to die, when you're as old as I am."

Mr. Silveira smiled. "You're talking like a fool, Tomé! And you know it. Why, seeing you drive down the street, the way you got off the truck . . ." lifting his hand to halt his friend's reply, "Oh, I know. You had a slight heart attack. You were told to be careful. The point is, you are. I tell you, you'll live to be a hundred."

Madruga shrugged his shoulders. "You, of course, know Luis Sarmento. Know what he's done so far. He wants to become somebody in America and this is good. What I want is to make sure he will really succeed after I'm gone. Do I make myself clear?"

"Yes," Mr. Silveira agreed.

"Now you understand why I came in so early. Our minds must be clear to work together."

Silveira nodded. "Let us get down to business, then."

"To begin with, I have no relations, nobody. They say when you die in America alone the state or maybe it's the county, moves in, takes your money, lands, all you've got. Not even enough is left for a Mass for your soul." The old man waited, then continued, "Unless you make a paper of some sort, and . . ."

"A will, yes," Mr. Silveira agreed. "First, you find out what you want to do with your property, ask a lawyer to write it down, sign before two witnesses and that's that."

"I see."

"In a will you have to appoint somebody to do as you would have done in life."

"And whoever does it will have to be paid?"

"Yes. Come to think of it, a lot of people: the executor, that's the one who will do the errands; the undertaker; the lawyer; the newspaper that will print some kind of notice after you're gone; the bonding company; and finally the state and the federal government in case you leave too much."

The old man took a long breath and closed his eyes a few moments. "We'll start with the ranch, then. Let's see, I intend to sell Luis Sarmento one-half of it, no favors—a fair price and a fair rate of interest. Half of the cows are his now, or soon will be." Again the old man waited, thinking. "This means I will only have half the ranch and half of the cows to dispose of, not to mention a few dollars in Romano's bank."

"That's true," Mr. Silveira agreed.

"Well, then," the old man said, "we'll let the will go for now. What's important is Ana and her desertion." Mr. Silveira nodded. "A poor green girl, alone in this big land, no English, nothing."

"Her man failed to appreciate her, but I understand he was peculiar in his ways."

"Yes. I'm ashamed to mention what he asked Ana to do. Thank God she had the courage to refuse." Mr. Silveira nodded. "This explains the real reason for my visit so early. I mean, what must this girl do? She can't go on like this."

"Ana should divorce this man," Mr. Silveira said.

"But the Church? Remember we live in a Catholic community."

"Of course, the Church may in some cases annul the marriage. Why don't you talk it over with our priest? But I must warn you, the wheels of Rome move slowly. Before this happens, if at all, it may take a long time. Months, even years."

"I know," the old man agreed. "Have you been taking notes of what we've been discussing?"

"Yes. So far you've gone from one thing to another, talked about this or that, and the way I see it you haven't come to any conclusion. I don't think you're ready to do business, as they say in America."

"That's true," Madruga agreed. Now, smiling quizzically he continued, "But I believe time will soon provide us with an answer. Now I can only think of this girl's freedom."

"Suppose I see a lawyer, then? Will it be all right?"

"Yes. Do that by all means," Madruga said. The old man got up and left the office just as the first bus drove by on its way to school.

The best time to discuss important matters, they knew, was always after supper. Luis remained at his place by the table while Ana put the dishes away, trying to be as noiseless as possible.

Without being told, Mr. Aguiar seemed to guess his presence in the kitchen was not wanted at this time. He got up and said, "If you don't mind, I'll take a walk tonight, see what's new in Pamplona." Anticipating the offer of a ride, he said, "No lift from anybody tonight. My legs, I've got to exercise them a little." He filled his pipe and lit it. "Goodnight, everyone. I'll be back by ten."

Now silence ensued. The old man broke it: "According to my figures, Luis, you'll have your contract paid in full in a few months. Not bad, eh?" The young man nodded.

"You don't even get excited, *rapaz*. I say again, what is happening to you?"

It was then Ana, sitting beside Luis, said, "May I say something, Tio?"

"Wait. I am concerned about this boy. He isn't the same anymore. I want to know why."

"What I'm about to say concerns Luis, myself and you, too, Tio."

"Ana, wait."

"If I speak, you'll understand what causes Luis' concern."

The old man seemed to be observing the young people across the table for the first time. He saw Ana's anxiety, Luis' confusion and desperation. The sweat of guilt was on his face.

"Go ahead, girl," Madruga said. Through the screened window the air seeped in, cool, smelling of that last hay cutting. A farmer's moon, big and yellow, shone in the sky behind a clump of willows. "This should be a fine night to sleep," the old man thought.

"As far as I know, there is only one way out. I'll leave the ranch." This was not what Ana wanted to say and the old man guessed it.

"Let it all come out, girl."

"Don't be foolish, Ana," Luis said, "What I mean is I will leave. Somewhere, I've heard of Nevada, not so many people out there. Perhaps we could come to some kind of settlement, Tio and I. We might cancel our contract. Enough to sustain me until I find something. I want no more." Pausing, his voice betrayed his emotion. "If there is anyone in need of help and direction, it is Ana. You see, I love her."

"A lot of things are clear now," Madruga seemed to be speaking to himself. "This boy and his silences; the way he went about his chores. Money, he did not care how much he had left at the end of the month. He should have known love and business do not go together too well. It's either one or the other. You didn't even guess that I, an old bachelor, knew anything about matters of the heart, did you? And perhaps you're right."

A glance from Luis encouraged Ana to continue. "I'm going to have a baby, Tio." This was the most direct way. Tell all your troubles in a single sentence if possible, then wait.

Madruga spoke quite calmly. "I better consult Mr. Silveira—as soon as possible. I have found the solution and I know what to do."

103

"Whatever you decide, Tio. I'm willing to go. Ana needs you and surely you must need her. As I said, I'm just another milker. I can easily be replaced." Yet, if the old man agreed to his banishment, yes, that was the right word, would that solve anything?

"You will stay here, boy, and you, girl. This is your home. You better get used to the idea."

"We're repaying kindness with trouble," Ana said. "You, who have lived a respectable life in this colony . . ."

"I know," said the old man, "and it does not matter. What is important, more important than ever, is the divorce."

"Divorce?" Ana asked.

"It's the American way to undo a bad thing. It will set you free after a time. As for you, Luis, all I can say is leave this girl alone after today. Wait until a judge says she is free to marry again. We must avoid a scandal for the sake of the child."

"Yes, Tio."

"And, of course, this is Linhares' child." He added quickly, "For its sake it will have to be."

"Tio . . ." Luis began.

"I won't listen, boy. Later, yes, later we will correct many things but for the present . . ." The old man took a large handkerchief from his trousers' back pocket and wiped his eyes. "Of course, we will have to see Dr. Barboza tomorrow. It's the right thing to do, or so I've been told."

"So early, Tio?" Ana wondered.

"Barboza will examine you. A baby must be a serious business. Should you really go on working after tonight?"

Ana smiled. "I feel fine, Tio. Why, in our island women worked in the fields, did what must be done up to a day or so before delivery. True, isn't it?"

"This is America," Madruga said. "You do what the doctor says you must. If he says take it easy . . ." He waited a moment. "I think I'll go to bed early this evening and think. Goodnight."

In the darkness of his room, Madruga felt a little disappointed and hurt. It would have been so much better had the boy remained as he was in the beginning—in love with the farm and what it meant to his future. Then he would have been proud of this green one who had done what he himself had done. Then, later, he could have looked around a bit and married a serious woman, a good cook, and, of course, one conscious of the value of a dollar. Too soon Luis had gone the way of those who listened to de Castro's sweet talk.

Now Ana was pregnant, deserted by a man who could return at any time and who, on his discovery of her condition, could, unjustly in a way, proclaim her a *puta*, no less.

What would the colony say? It was strange—up to now he had not concerned himself too much with his neighbors' affairs. As far as he knew, they were as normal as anybody, going about their daily work, marrying, having babies, burying their dead. Scandals were rare, and when these took place . . . he recalled Maria dos Cedros fifteen years before.

There was an army camp near Pamplona then and on weekends the soldiers used to come to town, and there were dances, walks and rides to the countryside. When the camp was closed, and the soldiers left, it was found that Maria was pregnant, and on learning of it her father ran her out of the house, as it was done in the old country years ago, and there was not a single Portuguese who offered to help the poor girl. He himself had been one of those who had seen her severed head beside the railroad track! She had chosen to kill herself instead of listening to the accusing voices of the colony.

Well, he, Madruga, may as well be ready for what was coming his way. All he needed was a few years of good health and a sharp tongue to silence the critics. After all, he did not owe anybody anything. He felt his pulse carefully as Dr. Barboza had told him to do whenever he felt or thought he felt a little excited: his heart seemed to mark the time as always, an even, strong beat.

Dr. Barboza asked his patients to come in early, and this morning Madruga and Ana were the first to arrive at his office. He greeted them curtly, motioning them to follow him to the first aid room.

"Come," the doctor said, "it won't cost you less if you stand." He said to Madruga, "How is the old pump making out?"

"Oh, that," the old man finally understood. "Fine, fine, doctor."

"No more racing all over the field like crazy, eh?"

Madruga shook his head. "Nothing like that, doctor. But I feel like it, sometimes."

"Don't think I'd call you a fool if you did, even though you'd be one, naturally. Matter of fact, I myself would like to close this office for a week or two and go to the mountains. I'd like to fish every day, walk a lot, do crazy things, but I won't, and that's why you were a foolish but brave man. What if you did run the risk of dying?"

"How true, doctor."

Dr. Barboza paused a moment. "I suppose you came here for a check up? Or is it the girl?"

"It's Mrs. Linhares, doctor."

"I see." Smiling, now appraising the young girl facing him, "Do you know I'd give anything to be twenty-five again? Isn't she pretty, old man?"

Madruga nodded. "It's all right, Ana. He talks like that."

Dr. Barboza became all business again. "Well, what is the matter?"

"The girl thinks she is pregnant, doctor. Go ahead, Ana."

"She is, eh? What a pretty young woman should be. Go ahead, Mrs. Linhares."

"I'll wait outside, doctor."

"You'd better. We've got to be sure of our young woman's condition," the doctor said.

Madruga nodded, addressing Ana. "This is the way things are done in America. You must be examined in the beginning. For one thing, you must have a healthy baby—no complications."

"Good morning, Mrs. Leal." The old man found his neighbor waiting to see Dr. Barboza. Suddenly the thought came to him that he wished he had not seen this woman here, and in this way postpone the eventual shock of the discovery, by the housewives of Pamplona, of Ana's condition. Women, after all, were women; their words could build a mountain from a single phrase if passed along at the right time.

Mrs. Leal said, "It's terrible to be getting old. Here I am, my piles are killing me. I just hope the doctor will not recommend an operation." Then, in a lower voice, she continued, "Is he in good humor this morning? He's fine and all that, but I just shake all over when I come here. The way he talks, sometimes."

"That's his way. Myself, I'm no Saint Anthony, either. Like everybody, I have my own bad days."

An uneasy silence ensued and Mrs. Leal began again: "Like I said, it's terrible to be old and here we stay, me and my old man, passing the days all by ourselves. In a way, it's good. To see our boys and girls driving around like mad, all by themselves, nobody to watch over them; and we hear of terrible things happening once in a while. It wasn't like that in the Old Country. There the first man to know a girl would be her husband, thanks to the Virgin. Not so here."

"We must go with the times, neighbor. Time and place. Sometimes, no matter how hard you try . . ." He thought of Ana momentarily, hoping her examination would not take too long.

"For one thing," Mrs. Leal said, "we do have a clean colony here. Our Portuguese are afraid of the Lord, and that is good." She paused and then said, "But I have heard of a place in town, and there for a fee, women of sin wait. Why our husbands *prefer* that to their wives is beyond me. I'm not forgiving our young boys. They should marry, and if that is not possible, a lot of hard work should keep them away from sin." Mrs. Leal changed her sitting position, saying, "Really, my piles are killing me."

It was then Ana walked out from the consultation room, followed by Barboza, who, unmindful of Madruga and Mrs. Leal, continued to talk. "The important thing is your diet," he said. "Follow it. Don't go on eating a lot, or before you know it you'll be giving birth to a ten pound baby." He waited a moment. Come and see me once a week." Then he said to Madruga, "And you?"

"I said it, doctor. I feel fine."

"Take those pills, then. No hard work. No worries."

"Yes, sir," said the old man.

"I'll examine you again when our young mother comes in." After a pause he continued. "She is pretty, isn't she?" To Mrs. Leal he said, "The same thing, I suppose?"

She nodded. Then she smiled and said to Ana, "I heard, *filha*. I couldn't help it. Congratulations." Her smile was a precise, measured smile, already tainted with malice.

"Why we had to run into that busybody," Mr. Madruga said to Ana as they drove home, "I don't know. It just goes to show, you can't keep a secret from people too long. Anyway, why not? Now tell me about the doctor."

"He was very kind," Ana said.

"You did not discuss the paternity, did you?"

"No, Tio," Ana said. "But I will when I go back next week. It's proper."

"Very good. Now I will go and see Mr. Silveira. We must consult a lawyer. The way I understand it, you may even be able to get an annulment. What is important is that you be free from Linhares as soon as you can. Unless you want to go back to José?"

"Oh, no, Tio. Please."

"A divorce or an annulment, then. You'll marry Luis and that's the end of the matter."

"And the child?"

"He is your child, isn't he? That is all that matters now." They had reached the yard and the old man said, "Fix a little lunch for the men. I won't be here. And take it easy." He turned the pickup around and drove away.

"Whatever lawyer you suggest," Madruga said, "as long as he is honest and won't rob anybody."

"There's a new one, just graduated, likely hungry, at the county seat," Mr. Silveira said, "and I have a surprise for you. His name is Gabriel Freitas."

The old man smiled a little, scratching his beard. "Is he . . ."

"He is," Mr. Silveira said. "As Portuguese as we are, or as his name. He is proud of his race, unlike so many of us. You know what I mean, those who change as soon as they can speak English well enough to get by, who look down on those of us who cannot. They're ashamed of our week-old beards, our overalls spattered with manure, our unpolished ways, our backwardness, even our fear. He is not like some of us who possess great leadership, who must be at the head of the table, the speechmakers, those who carry their rosaries above their heads as they approach the communion rail, so that all may see how friendly they are with God. What I want to say is our Mr. Freitas is a man like you or me, able and willing to do whatever he can for his client, for a modest fee."

"Let's go and see him," Madruga said.

Mr. Freitas' office was above the firehouse, a modest room simply furnished. The furniture consisted of a desk, a few chairs and a filing cabinet. A set of codes lay on his desk within easy reach. Mr. Freitas was in and he got up at once, greeting Mr. Silveira and turning to Madruga, he waited, an open smile on his dark, boyish face.

"This is Tomé Madruga, an old friend," Mr. Silveira said.

"Sit down," the lawyer invited. "You must excuse the office. I was admitted to the bar six months ago and decided to start by myself. This is a good town, a lot of our own people live around here and so . . ."

His shirt was open at the collar, a sport coat and slacks completed his dress. "Sometimes I wonder if I'd have done better had I stayed at the ranch." He smiled toward Mr. Silveira. "My father wanted me to be a great man, a lawyer, no less, and here I am. So far I've handled a few cases. I've made enough to pay the rent and eat."

"Mr. Madruga, you're a dairyman, aren't you?"

"Yes."

"Sometimes I crave the smell of the barn, all that dry hay inside of it and all those animals lined up waiting."

It was then that Madruga noticed his hands, developed by years of hard work, and he said, "I have, living in my home, a girl whose husband left her after working for me a few months. She is young, a fine cook, and wants to stay on the ranch. The way I figure, she should divorce her husband."

"Why?" Mr. Freitas asked.

"Because he is no damn good and, worse still, he's old enough to be her father."

Mr. Freitas smiled: "I suppose desertion is as good a ground for divorce as any. Her husband must be served with the papers, of course. Where is he?"

Madruga shrugged his shoulders.

"Either personally or by publication, the defendant must know."

"You go ahead and draw up the papers," Madruga said.

"Are you sure her man can't be located? It would make things a lot easier."

"He used to talk of going down to San Diego, tuna fishing. That was his dream. For all I know, he might be in some boat approaching Guatemala or Panama."

"I see." Mr. Freitas waited. "I'll prepare the complaint. Which reminds me, an uncontested divorce such as this should be worth one hundred and twenty-five dollars."

"Here's my checkbook," Mr. Madruga said. "Write it out." The old man wrote his signature in a slow hand, each letter an effort for him to write.

"Have Mrs. Linhares come in in the morning, and thanks. Many thanks."

"Descending the stairway, Madruga told his friend, "Do you know, I like this fellow a lot. You talk to him and you know he is as sound as a dollar before the Depression. What a milker he'd turn out to be at the ranch! Those hands . . ."

He noticed at once as he entered Corvello's accompanied by Mr. Silveira, a short silence ensued. It was as if all the card players had suddenly lost their voices, as if they were exposed to two strangers, entering the smoke-filled room.

But it did not last too long. A man at the counter suddenly got up and walked up to the old man, greeting him in a loud and happy voice. It was Garcia, the suit vendor.

"How was that *roupa*?" he asked. "I just know it fitted fine. I'll bet every woman looked at you twice. Mr. Silveira, I've called on your friend a steady thirty years, and finally I was able to outfit him. It goes to show, keep at something, keep at it a long time, selling goods or courting a girl, and eventually you'll strike the gold you're after."

"What are you doing here, and so early?" Madruga asked. "This is winter."

Garcia laughed. "It must be your age, old man. Don't you know my route begins in San Diego? I must start early down there and move on up slowly." Madruga nodded. "And Pamplona being a kind of midway point in my travels, it's only natural that I stop here and have a meal with my friends." Laughing, he said, "And there is always a little gossip to listen and carry along." Mr. Garcia paused. "Why don't we find a table and eat? I was about to." Madruga hesitated. "Come. It's on me. I feel good at this time of year."

While they were being served, Tio Corvello stopped a moment to whisper to Madruga. "When you finish, come to the back room."

The old man queried his friend with his eyes. "In the back. After you eat."

Meanwhile the men stopped by Garcia's table, shook hands or slapped his back, laughing, calling him a crook, saying, why, he'd sell them burlap, anything, it made no difference what and the prices! Mother of God!"

Mr. Garcia, knowing his clients, agreed with them, saying what they had paid last year was really nothing, they'd pay a lot more this season and gladly; surely they wanted to look just so during the *festas*.

111

While the loud talk was going on, Madruga wondered why his neighbors seemed to be so distant in their behavior towards him. Was this on account of Ana's condition? He found out, after lunch.

"You may as well know," Corvello said. "Our dairymen are puzzled. They don't quite understand why Ana should be pregnant when as a matter of knowledge . . ."

"It's none of their business," Madruga said.

"They feel it is," Corvello said. "I've just heard someone talk about it. The honor of the colony is again at stake. The only one serious scandal they had was when that girl, you remember a few years back, and now here's a married woman whose husband suddenly leaves, who refuses to follow him and now finds herself pregnant. Whose child is it? Tomé, this kind of talk in our colony is very bad."

The old man got up. "I have nothing to say. You have said everything so far. Let the gossips find the answer."

"They will," Corvello said. "The way I see it, we were a good colony living together, all of us, doing good in America, and I think you should do your part and clean house."

"Let's go, Mr. Silveira," Madruga said, getting up. "Corvello, I'm really surprised to hear you talk like this."

"I'm your friend, meaning no harm, Tomé. Now the others . . ."

The old man walked out, straight as a rod, his gray beard bristling, looking neither to left nor right.

"*Canalhas*," he said to Mr. Silveira, when they were outside. "Yes, that's what they are. Why, here I've been practically all my life—pay my taxes, go to church a lot more than I used to, and above all else, I mind my own business. Just because I have befriended two young people, who need me more than ever."

Madruga shouldn't be too upset, considering his problems, Mr. Silveira told him in his own quiet way. He lived too much within himself. And if the truth were known, if one lived in a Portuguese colony one must be a part of it, take an active part in all those little things which keep it together. Go to Church, attend the feasts, read a Portuguese paper to keep abreast of all the happenings here and in the lands on the other side, and Tio had not done all this; he had indeed been too busy building his own little kingdom, and now that he had tasted the finer things of life, the laughter of the young in the house, smelling now of new paint, singing with light, comfortable with new furniture—he should also know the possible sorrow that a sudden change could bring.

"I've minded my own business," Madruga's answer seemed to explain all matters to Mr. Silveira. "Ana and Luis have not done anything to anybody. Why must our people interfere?"

"They haven't yet," Mr. Silveira said. "For now, will you do yourself a big favor? Go home, eat a little and go to bed early. It'll do you a lot of good, and I don't have to be a doctor to know that. Come to think of it, you've done a good day's work so far. Ana's divorce is ready to file. By the way, one year is not too long to wait for freedom, is it?"

"Whenever I think of that bunch at the pool hall, their silence . . . I'll fight them all, I tell you."

In bed, Ana brought him a glass of milk, to which she had added a little sugar and cinnamon. He drank it slowly, showing his gratitude and pleasure by a prolonged smile.

"How were things at the ranch today?" he asked her teasingly.

"Luis did the usual things, followed your orders. We didn't even speak."

"No complaints?"

"No, Tio."

"Good." Then he said, "But I know better. Had he done that, I'd send him away tomorrow. Not that I know a thing about this nonsense called love, still . . ." Ana laughed.

Then he told her about his trip to Mr. Freitas' office, and said, "Goodnight, daughter," in a whisper. Ana left the room, closing the door noiselessly after her.

113

Mrs. Leal did not mind the doctor's admonition. For the moment she had forgotten her ailments. What she wanted most was to get home as soon as possible in order to make a few telephone calls. "It just goes to show," she thought while the doctor wrote her prescription, "you can't sin too long without being caught."

"For one thing, you are still overweight, you've got to quit eating bread and drinking milk the way you do. Oh, a slice of bread and a glassful is all right but . . ."

"Yes, doctor."

"Do this for a whole month."

Driving back, Mrs. Leal felt excited, breathing the cool air of winter. The beginning scandal gave her a certain pleasure, for it was she who had discovered it, and it would be she who would, with her friends, help bring it to the fore. It would be her duty to do it: anyone else in the colony would do the same thing, and gladly. The fear of God demanded it. It had always been the same in the Old Country. A woman was married to one man forever. Your husband was a wall jumper? You prayed for deliverance and suffered in silence. But Ana Linhares? Mrs. Leal concluded, no matter what the excuse, Ana could not—again her judgment, or rather her supposition, could be without foundation. It was a natural thing for a woman to become pregnant eventually—if married. Age was no barrier, if one was to take her man's age into consideration, yet—she recalled what they used to say about Linhares, from his own wife's mouth, come to think about it.

Mrs. Leal walked into her kitchen and sat at the table near the window. The telephone was nearby and the first call was completed. "Mrs. Lucas?" she began, and there were others. Mrs. Costa and Mrs. Ferreira were eventually called. "I baked a few loaves of sweet bread yesterday, and the coffee is about done. Come on over. Some news? Yes."

It was pleasant in Mrs. Leal's kitchen. The sun, quite bright, accentuated the green of the alfalfa fields soon to be burned by the season's first frosts. Pamplona's dairymen were beginning to complain of a near drought. Quince fruit hung listlessly yellow from a tree in the center of the yard. Mrs. Leal thought the time was near to harvest the fruit and turn it into jam.

First to arrive was Mrs. Lucas, a tall, thin-nosed woman, whose single red pimple on the left nostril gave the impression that she was suffering from a cold. She spoke in a whimpering way, as if with a perpetual hurt within.

"I don't know what is the matter, neighbor," Mrs. Lucas said in greeting. "I just don't feel good. It must be these cold mornings; my feet are like ice all night. My husband threatens to leave our bed and sleep in the bunkhouse."

"Come, have a little coffee, neighbor," Mrs. Leal urged.

Mrs. Lucas noticed the platter full of sweet bread on the table. "I just know it will taste so good. You've always been a good baker."

"Oh, I try to be," Mrs. Leal agreed, "but it will be a waste of my time from now on. I've just come from the doctor, and do you know what he said? I'm too fat; I must not have anything rich, milk and sweet bread, for one."

It was then Mrs. Ferreira walked in, accompanied by Mrs. Costa. "What is it, *filha*? No bad news from the Old Country?"

"Ah, the Old Country," Mrs. Leal said wistfully. "I don't think too much about our islands these days. My parents are dead, God keep them in Heaven. I have no brothers, no sisters." She smiled. "But memories do come back, now and then. The fine teachings of my mother, for instance. Her warnings before I came to America." Mrs. Leal assumed a certain mysterious tone as she said, "I wish all parents had talked to their children about the dangers of sin in this big land." After a moment she added, "I know of a case where these warnings were not given. Come, sit, all of you. Let's have a little coffee and bread."

The women sat clumsily and at once began to discuss their various ailments and diets. "I just don't understand it," Mrs. Costa said. "We came to this country to have our fill of good things, and now the doctors tell us, 'You can't do this or that thing. This out, no fat on your steak, eat dry toast.' Life isn't worth living anymore. Good thing we still can see each other once in a while to gossip a little."

"I must say of late we have had little to gossip about; we pay our bills, go to Church, buy a new dress at Penney's now and then . . ." Mrs. Ferreira, as usual, accepted life without complaint and certainly without hope of change.

Now Mrs. Leal said, "Today I overheard, quite by accident, some news that should excite us a little. I'll be direct: I was in Barboza's office waiting to see him, and out of his consultation room comes none other than Ana Linhares. *Filhas*, the girl is pregnant! I heard it."

"She is young, isn't she? Even if her husband—I mean, a man of fifty can still do it." Mrs. Lucas soaked a slice of bread in the hot coffee.

117

"Oh, I understand," Mrs. Ferreira said. "I should know. I sleep with an old man and no amount of refusal—it's a cross we must carry."

Mrs. Leal smiled. "It isn't age in this case, *filhas*. Have you forgotten what Ana has been saying up to a few days ago? The old man's explanation of Linhares' sudden departure from the ranch? Well, I remember. He was a brute, yes, a man who had no desire for women, yes. Madruga said he had never touched the girl as a man." Here Mrs. Leal made the sign of the cross to ward off the devil. "A *maricas*—that's what Ana said her man was."

"If that is true," Mrs. Lucas began cautiously, "if that is true, the pregnancy means the child is not José Linhares'." This sudden, unexpected conclusion left Mrs. Lucas quite upset. "Blessed Lady!" she said, "We shouldn't be too hasty in our judgments. After all, how do we know Linhares is like *that*?"

It was then Mrs. Ferreira said, "If the child is not Linhares', who is the father? I haven't seen the girl anywhere. Always on the ranch, and a lot more since the old man is sick. Surely . . . It can only be her husband's."

Then Mrs. Costa laughed. "Luis Sarmento? Oh, no."

"Why not?" Mrs. Leal said. "He is young, isn't he? Does he ever go anywhere? Have you ever seen him go to our dances or Church functions?"

Mrs. Ferreira shook her head. "We shouldn't be too hasty in condemnation, really. Luis is a good boy. Has a good business head. Look at what he has accomplished so far. When your arms and legs are used in hard work, you forget the sweetness of sin."

Mrs. Leal said, "I'm going to watch this girl. If the child arrives too late, say one year after Linhares' departure, we would know the worst, wouldn't we?" Mrs. Leal thought a moment and continued, "If it comes in the usual time, knowing as we know the *maricas* of her husband ..." Mrs. Leal helped herself to a slice of bread and concluded, "The answer would be the same, wouldn't it?"

"That boy, eh?" Mrs. Ferreira said. "How strange. One never knows what makes us do what we do, and when you are alone . . . It's easy to be tempted, easy to fail."

Mrs. Leal said, "One thing we must do, try to prevent scandal in our colony. We are proud of our record, except for that one who killed herself. I mean, Ana Linhares should be approached and asked to leave."

"But *filha* . . ." Mrs. Costa began.

"We've lived here a long time; we should enforce our own rules. We have no room for *putedo* in Pamplona." Mrs. Leal was quite emphatic about this.

"Have you considered Madruga? Everyone knows how much he has learned to depend on Luis and Ana. A sick man besides."

"There are hospitals well equipped to care for old people. He is putrid with money; he could hire a team of doctors." Mrs. Leal paused. "The thing to do is to appoint a committee—we'd be it—and call at Madruga's as soon as possible."

"This would be a rather silly thing," Mrs. Lucas said. "Even if this boy and girl . . . this is America. You see, you can't bring about night justice, the way it was done in the Old Country."

Finally the women got ready to return to their homes. "Let's be prudent," Mrs. Lucas said. "Let us watch developments, but no action, not until we know."

Mrs. Leal smiled slightly, watching her neighbors leave. Across the road she saw Luis plowing a field. She heard the tap-tap-tap of the tractor and above the noise the sound of a whistle long and mournful, announcing twelve o'clock. Slowly she walked to the stove and lit it under a potful of kale soup for her husband's dinner.

Ana Linhares signed the divorce papers, and the following week a copy of the summons was printed in the *Pamplona Clarion*. No one expected Linhares to appear, much less contest it.

Mr. Freitas explained to Mr. Madruga, "You see, the girl will have to wait a year before the divorce becomes final. After that she may marry."

"She is going to have a baby," the old man said uneasily, as if that bit of news was something he did not care to discuss.

"It's too bad," Mr. Freitas said. "What I mean is, her husband's whereabouts being unknown, we can't force him to support the child and its mother."

"Oh, she won't starve," Madruga said. "As long as I'm around no one should worry about the girl."

"Anyway," Mr. Freitas said, "I've taken some precautions. If Linhares shows up anywhere in the county, the police will grab him. You just can't walk out on your wife, leaving her with child."

"A year passes like nothing," Madruga was talking to Ana and Luis that morning. "Still, the wait will be hard on you two. I mean, the gossip. Our colony is now cool towards me and will continue being so to all of us." The old man paused a moment. "What our Portuguese don't know is that I'm not too sick to put up a battle. Words, yes, and if necessary a two-by-four." Smiling, "I hope it won't come to that."

"It won't," Luis said. "No one has anything against you. You haven't bothered anyone."

"The colony is proud of its record, boy. No scandals to speak of in years."

"I've said, Tio, if things develop to such an extent that it might be better for us to leave . . ."

"You are staying, *rapaz*, no matter what happens. Do you understand?"

"Oh, why didn't I—I should have followed Linhares," Ana said.

"Don't ever talk like that again. Luis, shouldn't you go and see how our cows are doing? The calves, too. Feed them good. You've got to care for them when they're young."

"I'll go to the barn now."

"Yes, don't mind the rain; it's good for you." He laughed. "Rain means feed, better production. You want to be the owner of a healthy herd, the finest in Pamplona?" Before Luis could answer he said, "Why, your love trouble is nothing!" He watched Luis walking bareheaded outside.

"You see," he said to Ana, "That's the way I want him to be, alert—

working, ready." After a time he said, "Let the women talk if they wish. If the men feel different toward me, let them."

Ana said nothing, sitting at the table, her head resting on her hands.

It began as an evil flame one Sunday morning as they left the Church. No words were spoken; there were searching looks instead directed to Ana. It was evident the women were looking for signs denoting beginning of motherhood.

"Is her belly showing?" Mrs. Leal continued to be the leader of her group of moral gossips.

"Too early yet," Mrs. Costa said. "A few more weeks and then . . ."

"If it had been her husband's, he left some two months ago, we'd certainly be able to tell," Mrs. Leal said.

"*Bom dia, senhora,*" Mrs. Lucas greeted Ana. "Have you heard from your husband? When is he coming back?"

"I don't care to see him again," Ana said.

"He is, after all, the father of your child," Mrs. Leal said. "When he knows of your state . . ." Ana did not answer, waiting. It was then that Luis approached, followed by Madruga. "What is it?" he asked.

"Nothing," Ana said. "Are you ready to go?"

"Yes," the old man said. "What have you been talking about?" Before she could answer he said, "Oh, I know. Our neighbors have been questioning you. Have you satisfied their curiosity? You should. You're going to have a baby. You are divorcing your husband. What else do they want to know? Come along."

"Neighbor, I only said . . ." Mrs. Leal began. "I didn't say anything. But I might and very soon, I think."

The men parted a little to let them pass. They seemed embarrassed and a little guilty perhaps. They had listened to their wives, had perhaps agreed with them insofar as the awful scandal was concerned.

Mr. Lucas addressed Madruga. "How are you, Tomé? Take care of your pump. Don't be in a hurry to leave us." The other men smiled, nodding their assent.

At home, finally the old man said, "I'm driving back to Corvello's. There's a few matters I want to clear up, in a friendly way, I hope."

"I'll go with you, Tio."

"Not yet, boy. For now there's the ranch to attend to."

"Milking, yes. By the way, we should go and see Mr. Romano tomorrow. It's payday, isn't it."

Now they were finally alone; self-imposed silence or as much of it as possible, came between them. They behaved quite stiffly, as if they did not know each other very well. It was so difficult, for passion was there, burning.

"Ana," Luis began, and then he recalled the promise to the old man that for a prescribed time he must not touch this lovely, willing girl.

"What I wanted to say," Luis began, "tomorrow, if I figure it right, I'll be the owner of one-half of Tio's dairy, animals and equipment. Under the circumstances, I should be very happy, but I am not. The cruelty of the colony suddenly turned against us; Madruga has never hurt anyone. So, you see, being a man of property does not taste as sweet as I thought it would."

"This will pass, Luis," Ana said. "We will live it through. Let our women talk. They must. I'm one of them." The smile on her face did not dispel her worry. "As long as I'm sure of you . . ." Her hands made as if to reach his across the table.

"And I of you," Luis said. "Oh, just to know, the women are talking, and are calling you a *puta*. I just know it!"

"Am I not?" Ana retorted. "And proud of it in a way. Let my looks of sin say it, yet we're only behaving as two people in need of each other. We met at the right moment. Did you know of Linhares' strange behavior? My revulsion at being near him, commanded to do degrading things?"

"Ana, forget it."

"No, I want to talk. You were always a good listener, remember?" Luis nodded. "The way I felt, disgusted—lost in this big land."

"I tempted you. I should have waited."

"Be untrue to yourself? Our Day of Judgment will come. I know God will understand." Then, getting up, she said, "Oh, I almost forgot lunch! Come to think of it, Aguiar is in Pamplona and so is Tio."

Luis nodded. "Linguiça, eggs, potatoes, and coffee, good and strong. Can I make it?"

"Yes, first you set the table."

121

"I will, I will." Luis was feeling better.

"Just the same, this is a better land," Ana seemed to be weighing her present difficulties against the blessing of living in America. She said, "There we had nothing to eat; we had to wait for a saint's feast to enjoy something like a bit of salt pork, a chicken or a slice of white bread. If we could only free ourselves of the old customs, the jealousy and the malice."

"That's true," Luis agreed. "I must admit it, Tio is right. Time will cure all our troubles. We're young; we'll take whatever comes our way."

They drank the coffee very hot and in silence. Suddenly Luis asked, "Will it be a boy?" Then added, "But I'll accept whatever God sends us with pride." He paused. "Still, a son, to have a young boy by your side, the two of us together. This child, Ana, isn't it worth all the mean things the colony is saying about us?"

"Yes," Ana said. "But I want to be at peace. I need a good confession. Whatever I'm told to do as a penance, anything I will. Should I have debased myself, done what I was asked to do? Was that a part of the marriage contract?"

"Our new priest will listen. He is one of us, just arrived." He moved close to her, his arm tenderly about her. "You must not worry. What is the waiting of a few months? For us it will mean a son, and marriage."

"Marriage and baptism. Two ceremonies on the same day. We could do that." Ana smiled a little.

"A fine thought," Luis said. He lifted her up and kissed her. "Oh, my darling," he whispered. Then he remembered Madruga's dictum and walked out of the kitchen.

Tio Madruga especially had insisted that Ana accompany them to the bank the next morning. Mr. Romano saw them come in and opened the Madruga-Sarmento folder already on his desk. "I suppose this is our monthly visit, and you're ready to make the usual payment." Noticing Ana as she sat near Luis, he said with a knowing wink through his dark rimmed glasses, "Your girl, eh?"

"I hope to make her my wife," Luis said.

"Good! Congratulations." He spoke to the old man. "Now for the creamery checks and calf money, any cattle sold this month?"

"Yes," Madruga said. "Here, I have everything here." He handed an envelope to Mr. Romano. The banker added up the checks quickly. "And now the bills," he said.

Madruga produced another envelope and his commercial bank book. Mr. Romano began to write down the expense items. "Oh yes, State Oil Company, $28.30; Martin, the plumber, $18.13; Modern Garage, $12.90; R & R. Tractor $83.25—a new firm, isn't it?"

"A Portuguese firm," Madruga explained. "I understand they're very honest, stand by what they do. I mean, they guarantee their work."

"We need this in Pamplona. Integrity—to succeed one must have that."

"Congratulations, boy. Your contract is paid in full, and there is a two hundred dollar balance."

123

"I knew it," Madruga said, laughing. "You see, I didn't sleep last night figuring it out. I'm really proud, Mr. Romano. I've placed my trust in a fine, hard-working boy. I wasn't wrong, you see."

The banker pointed to a portrait of a handsome man, facing them. "Like you, he started without a cent, but he was willing to work and believed in his neighbors. One bank, yes; he began with one, and in a few years his name was well known all over California. He believed in security and credit, and respected both. And people. By this I mean one bank, and in your case, one passage fare. Then a dairy. And a tract of land; meanwhile you marry, have children. Later the children will take over and in the process some of us become wealthy, like Tomé Madruga."

Mr. Romano smiled. "I suppose you are ready to give a bill of sale to this young fellow?"

"I have it here," said the old man. "Luis, take care of your animals, feed them properly, as if you haven't been doing just that." His eyes became misty as he concluded, "I'm thinking of my first dairy and of how I bought it forty years ago. I paid for it the hard way; in those days we earned twenty dollars a month; we worked like horses; no tractors, milk machines, nothing. But I paid old Caetano the principal and interest. Funny thing, in those days there were no written contracts to keep you in line. You merely agreed on a price and that was that."

"Integrity," Mr. Romano repeated. "Shouldn't you leave some money with us, boy? After all, if you're going to marry, this is a good bank to start a savings account."

"Yes, sir," Luis agreed. He said to Ana, who had remained silent, unable to understand, "Mr. Romano suggests we start putting a little aside for the future."

"A good idea," Madruga interrupted. "You must have something ready whenever . . . You have guessed what is to come after this?"

"I have, Tio."

"Yes. The land, now that you are the owner of a share of the cattle. It's only natural we discuss the purchase of enough ground to feed one of these days."

Mr. Romano stood before his desk. "Remember now, whenever you're ready, we'll lend you whatever you need, providing, of course, you have enough security. As for our interest rates, we don't skin anybody, really."

Mrs. Leal and Mrs. Costa waited outside Penney's store watching Ana and Luis approach followed by the old man.

"Do you see what I see?" Mrs. Leal said in a low voice.

"Oh, yes," Mrs. Costa agreed. "Now it shows. She must be four months along, at least that."

And they smiled their precise, inconsequential smiles. "Without shame," Mrs. Leal said, following her friend into the store.

CHAPTER 13

Tio Corvello could hardly believe it, watching the man in all his big, unchanged flabbiness, sitting unconcernedly at the counter.

"Well!" he said, "Is it you? What are you doing here?"

"What else do you expect?" José Linhares said, and then added quickly, "Isn't this a free country? Can't a man come in or just pass by on his way somewhere? For one thing, I'm hungry. Bring me some food."

"I have some beans," Tio Corvello said, as if this was news to anyone.

"And bread, bring plenty of everything," Linhares said. "I'm hungry."

Corvello cut medium slices of French bread, seven or eight, which he placed before his customer. The beans came next, piping hot. "Butter?" he asked.

"Anything connected with a dairy, I mean the work, I hate. But butter, bring me plenty of it!" Then he was silent, soaking the bread in the thick bean gravy. He ate great mouthfuls rapidly.

Meanwhile, Tio Corvello watched. Linhares had not changed. He appeared as always, his clothes dirty, the large face unshaven. At least this was the way he used to come to town when employed at Madruga's ranch.

"Can you finish another bowl?" Corvello asked. "Go on, this one will be on the house."

Linhares granted his assent. "Do you know I didn't eat breakfast or lunch, just to come here and have my fill of these? Oh, by the way, is de Castro still around? I guess I need a shave and a bath."

"Oh, yes. You just can't do without Mr. de Castro. My beans and his barbershop. What would our Portuguese do without them?"

Linhares suddenly laughed. "You're right, old man. Which reminds me, I may just as well stay here overnight, unless the barber happens to be without something I crave. I mean girls," he said with his best lascivious smile. "Has he got any?"

Corvello waited a while, clearing the counter. "I hear of a new one, just arrived from Mexico."

"Expensive, eh?" Linhares asked.

Corvello shrugged his shoulders. "I'll be right back," José said, finally. "Oh, by the way, I'll pay you tomorrow morning for this and my breakfast. All right?" Without waiting for an answer, he was gone.

"What a strange man," Corvello thought. "Comes here, eats my food, thinks of pleasure at once and not a word about his wife. Has he any feelings left? And that child coming up. He behaved as if he didn't know anything about it, or didn't care."

Mr. Corvello went back to his favorite stool and to reading the *Portuguese Journal.*

José Linhares and his sudden appearance in Pamplona was taken up in great detail by Mr. de Castro, who on seeing the flabby man approaching, ran to the door and opened it with great flourish and warm greetings.

"It can't be possible," de Castro kept repeating. "Here's a good friend, one who has not forgotten. You've come back and it's good. I tell you, you're in luck all around. I'm going to fix you up, as the saying goes. First, a bath; the water is ready. Then a shave and the finest haircut I can give. Leave it to me, I know what to do."

"And then?"

De Castro laughed. "Then you want a room and a partner. Oh, wait until you see her." A pause and then he said, "You're not broke, are you?"

Linhares shook his head.

"Well then, let us get started."

Linhares sat in all his flabbiness in the tub filled with near-boiling water. "Here's a wash rag and a bar of soap. Do a good job on yourself."

When he began to shave him later, he asked in a careful way, "What I mean is, I am rather surprised to see you back after what happened. I mean, when a woman is young and her husband leaves her without a cause, or so she says; and when a woman feels her husband is not coming back, goes ahead and files for divorce . . . it's the American way, my friend, you know that . . ."

A hot towel covered Linhares' face at the moment. He answered through the opening near his nose. "You mean Ana went to court and asked that she be set free?"

"Yes, and do you know you've been in the papers at least three times? Week after week. The law says you've got to be told your wife is leaving you, and because no one knew where you were . . ." Mr. de Castro stropped his razor listlessly.

Linhares said, "Well, here I am, if anybody wants me. I'm not running away, and I'm telling you this, I asked Ana to come along. But no, she refused. And why? Hasn't a man the right to demand anything from a wife? Why marry a woman, if you can't use her the way you want to? I've got to pay good money to a stranger, too."

127

De Castro interrupted him. "It's funny, but a man's face clean of beard is always a pleasant sight. To me, at least. Conception should see you now. A big man like you. Go, go upstairs. I'll put you up for the night."

"And?"

"Yes, yes. That extra something will cost ten dollars. Like I said, this girl is really good. Experienced, that's what she is." He paused. "Oh, I just remembered, you'll find your room at the head of the stairs. On the right."

The barber stood by his empty chair a few moments. Then he walked to the door and looked up and down the street, almost deserted now. Dairymen were in their barns, milking. "May as well go up and close for the day," he thought, locking the front door. "I do hope this fool will stay a few days at least. Doesn't seem broke and Conception needs a few dollars to send the folks back home."

The next morning found Linhares at his most boastful self. "Oh, but I feel fine, my friend," he greeted the barber. "I tell you, you really have something upstairs. That girl, wow!"

"She'll be ready whenever you want her," de Castro offered, cautiously. "Your wife wasn't anything like that, eh?"

"What did you say? I tell you the *señorita* beats anybody!" Then, "Were you talking about my wife? I've forgotten all about her. She's nothing to me—nothing."

"Good. Especially now that she is about to have that baby."

"That's right . . ." Linhares did not finish the sentence. "Did I understand you to say my wife is . . . ?"

"Pregnant, yes. Or didn't you know?"

"Do you realize I've been away all these months?" Linhares got up ready to leave. "I think I'll walk to the Madruga ranch this morning. A short visit, naturally. I may as well congratulate Ana."

It was cold outside; the frost was now upon the land, softening the tall, dry grass along the road. As he walked on, a pickup approached and stopped. It was Mr. Leal. "Can't believe it. It's José. How are you?"

"Fine," Linhares said curtly.

"I suppose you're going over to the old man's. Want a ride? I'll turn around."

"No, I'll walk. I'm used to it." Although Mr. Leal wanted to continue the conversation, he thought he might as well go on about his affairs.

128 Meanwhile, Linhares was beginning to evaluate his own situation. If his wife was pregnant—a certain thing, of course, for de Castro had so informed him. How did it feel being a cuckold, walking to the place where his *puta* of a woman lived? It was that pride again. Yes, and a strange feeling of jealousy. Yes, it was that. If he himself had not . . . Ana had refused him. By rights, no one should have had her; and now he was being told of her pregnancy, and for all he knew he was being accepted as the father. Oh, this was a great joke, and the strangest thing of all was that at the moment he was not angry at anybody. It was just his pride. He had been hurt, yes. What would he say to his friends when the inevitable question would be asked? Throw out his chest and say, "Yes, I'm the father."

Mrs. Leal had evidently seen him from her kitchen window. He saw her by the gate as he came by.

"In the name of the Father . . ." the woman made the sign of the cross to show her excitement. "Is it you, José? What brought you here? Have you heard . . . ?"

"I have no time for you," Linhares said walking on. "I've got to go in there." Madruga's place seemed to be deserted. "Do you think they're home?" he asked, pointing across the road.

"Better control your temper," Mrs. Leal warned. "Remember, you're being looked for, the police will arrest you. You've left your woman, and now there's this baby and you've got to provide for it when it arrives."

But Linhares did not hear. He walked away and finally entered the familiar yard, saw the flower beds and vegetable patch. Approaching the steps, he paused a moment, feeling confused, and if anything, foolish. Here he was on the ranch where he had been discharged, about to face a woman who was still his wife, and all the things he had planned to say, the insults—now he did not know what to say to her.

He started to walk up and, as he did, the old courage and anger returned with each step. He knocked and the door shook. It was more than a mere knock. He was ready to push himself in, and he did. The door was unlocked. He saw Ana at once by the kitchen sink.

"Hello, José," she said.

Her voice hadn't changed at least. It was calm as always.

"Ana," Linhares began, "I want to talk to you."

"Talk," Ana said, "but don't come near me."

"Don't tell me what to do," Linhares said. He came toward her, almost touching her. "You are getting fat, aren't you? Tell me, how many months now?" He felt very calm, even though his pride and the idea of being near the woman he had desired in the only way he knew—his voice was harsh and very low, "Where is the old man and your stallion, Ana? Luis is the one, isn't he!"

"They're by the cotton willow field fixing a ditch box." At once Ana was sorry for having given him this information. Here she was alone with a man who might in a moment of anger harm her. "I must avoid an argument," she cautioned herself. "José," she said, "sit down. Yes, we will talk. Here, I'll drink some coffee with you."

"I'm not thirsty."

"*Por favor.*"

"I'll stand. Tell me, the whole town must know of your pregnancy. Who is the father, Ana? Whoever he is, he must be very special."

"What happened . . . I was alone, José. I fell in love. It was sinful and I knew it but I couldn't help myself."

"Your husband . . . you never loved me, Ana. I was the meal ticket. You wanted to come to America, and for that you would marry anybody, young or old!"

"Luis resisted as much as I."

"Where did it happen?" Linhares asked. "The horse barn! What a *puta* you turned out to be! What a shameless *puta*!"

"Get out! Whatever I am does not matter to you. I am divorcing you. Don't you understand?"

Now she knew the worst was about to happen. "I should kill you!" he said. He waited, looking outside. "I'm safe, you see. Your stallion

129

and the old fool are still out there; I can see them. Cry for help and I'll strangle you! Of course, if . . ." A sudden perverse thought began to direct his actions. He ripped her blouse and skirt. It was an easy task. His hands were all grip at the moment. He felt her in a rough caress, and now he pulled her face to his. He kissed her, a long kiss, taking her lips into his mouth as if he were chewing her. Then he pushed her away and whispered, "Kneel! Hurry up!" His hands circled her throat as she refused. They were like a vise around her throat while he entered, gradually into a state of ecstasy.

It was a strange pleasure mixed with revenge, pride and hatred. The idea that he could be caught, the idea that she was doing for the first time what he as her husband had been unable to make her do—now he wanted to tell her nice things, tell her he was ready to forgive her.

"You know how I am. This is my way." Suddenly he left her as she was, huddled on the floor, weeping softly. "I'm really sorry, *cachorra*." He ran down the steps and across the yard on his way to Pamplona. The bus to Sacramento would be arriving in half an hour; he'd be just in time.

But he could not avoid meeting Mrs. Leal again. She had waited, smiling. "José Linhares, come in a second. I have some coffee brewing."

He wanted to curse her, conscious of the time and the possibility of being caught. Ana could just as well call the police. "I'm in a hurry, I've got to be in Pamplona in a few minutes," he said.

Mrs. Leal saw his restlessness and decided to get whatever information she could while she could. "Some other time, then?" She waited a moment, then went on, "Anyway, you did see your wife and I'm sure she told you the good news. Aren't you proud of being a father?"

"Oh yes," José said. "Of course."

Mrs. Leal was as direct as she could be. "You are the father, aren't you?"

"There is doubt in this bitch's mind," Linhares thought. He remembered Ana huddled on the floor of the kitchen, fearful for her life, fearful of being caught performing what she considered sinful and degrading. Vengeance was now gone from him. Why publicly admit anything?

He said, "Don't you think I'm quite able to father a child? Bring me a woman: I'll show you." He leered intensely toward the surprised woman. "You ask Ana who the father is. As for you, are you sure you invited me to have a cup of coffee only? Only that? Come, let's go in." José laughed, showing his yellow teeth.

This had the desired effect. "Go away, man! Go and play with those *cabras* who are willing. I'm a respectable woman, don't you forget that." Mrs. Leal walked away without looking back. "But he isn't the father," she thought. "He didn't answer the question. Now I know."

Linhares left Pamplona without a trace. Corvello couldn't understand why, nor, for that matter, could de Castro. One held unpaid tags for meals and the other for a night's lodging; small amounts, to be sure, yet a principle of long standing had been violated. The Portuguese paid their bills, large or small.

Linhares' departure only meant one thing—he must have been in a great hurry to forget his obligations. The girl upstairs had been paid, and this in itself was fine. Conception was not expected to offer her services for nothing unless she was in love.

In less than a week the entire colony knew of Linhares' disappearance from the local scene. "You know, husband," Mrs. Leal addressed her man later, "it must have been me coming face to face with Linhares, the excitement of it, I mean. What I mean to say is that I feel a lot better now. I found out he is not the father. He told me to go and ask Ana, as if I were interested, which I am not. What husband would deny being the father of a baby if he wasn't? Who can enjoy being a cuckold, I ask you?" Mrs. Leal took a long swallow of cold milk and said, wiping her lips, "The father of this baby is Luis Sarmento. I'm going to tell the shameless girl this with my own mouth."

"Why must you, woman? We are neighbors, and besides, what happened there is no part of our concern. Who are we to meddle in other people's business?"

"It is *our* business, husband. As members in good standing in our colony. The two young ones are intruders; you know that. California is a big place, let them go elsewhere. We'll tell them to go. It's our duty."

"If they refuse? This is not the Azores, woman." Mr. Leal waited a moment, then he went on, "Remember Madruga's illness and how much he depends on Ana for help."

"Leave it to us women. We'll call on José's wife. We'll at least try to keep the good name of our people free of scandal."

"I want no part in this affair! It's all right to talk, but to go about telling people what to do is silly!"

"The time to act is now," Mrs. Leal seemed to be speaking to herself. "Act before the girl gets too big. That's one favor we'll be doing, asking her to leave while she still can in a quiet way."

"It's crazy," Mr. Leal said.

"We have an obligation. Now in the Old Country, it would have been different over there. Force could be used at night, but here, no. Just the same, we'll do what we can as good Christians." Mr. Leal grunted and walked away from the kitchen.

Ana saw Linhares leave, heard the front door bang and the sound of his steps fading away on the gravel. She got up slowly, gathered her torn clothes about her and went into the bathroom. She must bathe at once, wash her body in hot water. She felt unclean. She wanted to vomit, and she did by placing her finger deep into her throat. The thought of what she had been forced to do, the memory of José's rough fingers on her throat, the awful silence in the kitchen except for his moaning and grunting commands and finally his pushing her away in feral satiation—she would soap and rub thoroughly. How could she kiss Luis again? She could not forgive herself for her momentary understanding of this lost man—lost, she knew, through no fault of his own. Certain men were born like that, perhaps.

Now she was dry, clean again, her body at least clean. The thought came to her quite suddenly—should she call the police, charge Linhares? No. If she did, it would add to the scandal already afoot in the colony. She thought of the coming child.

She returned to the kitchen and began to prepare lunch. It had been a dream, an evil dream, finally gone. She must not think of it again. Luis must not even guess. Her oncoming motherhood would serve as a perfect excuse for her behavior. She prepared the food listlessly. Outside, the sun shone bright on all the land. She saw Luis and Madruga walking slowly towards the house. If only they had been at home an hour or so before!

But her mental state did not go unnoticed. Luis saw it first. Her movements, almost mechanical, her eyes trying to avoid his, the forced normalcy of her ways. At the end of the meal he finally asked, "What's the matter, Ana?"

"Nothing, nothing," she said quickly.

Madruga said, "Can't a girl about to have a baby cry if she feels like it? You have, haven't you?"

Ana remained silent throughout the rest of the meal. Then she said, "I've had a visitor this morning."

"Linhares?" Luis asked.

"Who gave him permission? Why did you let him in?" Madruga asked.

"The door was unlocked. He hasn't changed, Tio. He came here to see for himself, and cursed me. Oh, he said so many things."

"Did he touch you?" Luis began.

"He did not hurt me," Ana answered.

"Well! What did he do?" Madruga asked.

"He left after a while," Ana said. "He came in without warning, then left."

"Is he in town?" Luis asked.

"I'm sure he has gone. I don't believe he'll bother us. We won't see him again."

"Is he in Pamplona?" Luis insisted. "I'll have him arrested."

"Forget it, boy," Madruga said. "Linhares walked in on us, verified matters, then left. Yes, I think he's on his way."

Corvello told Madruga later, "José Linhares came in here, ate, went across the street for a haircut and a girl. Then he left this morning. Didn't pay me or de Castro. I understand he visited your place."

"Yes. Luis and I were in the field fixing a ditch box. He found his wife alone."

"Didn't harm her, did he?" Corvello asked. "I don't think he would. Does a lot of talking, threatens, but that's all."

Corvello laughed suddenly. "Do you know, our women aren't too happy about Ana's oncoming baby. They'd like to know who the father is."

"Does it matter?" Madruga asked. "What's important is that Ana will have a baby. To an old man it means something."

"I suppose you are right," Corvello said. "A young one—I tell you what, we'll have a little drink of my special Port in celebration of the coming event."

Madruga nodded. "I suppose Barboza would disapprove of it, but what is one to do?" After a pause he said, "I only hope I'll be here when it comes. To be a grandfather! I just know it will be quite a treat."

It was raining hard all over the valley. The clouds banked darkly above Pamplona, dark gray clouds, heavy with rain. It fell on the ground thickly and was absorbed very fast, since the weather had been dry. It was good to know that soon the fields would turn green, a sure promise of feed for the cattle.

The men watched the rain fall, listening to its music. Everyone was happy—merchants, dairymen, townspeople. The women sat by the windows in their kitchens, wrote letters to the Azores, listened to Portuguese programs on the radio, telephoned their neighbors and discussed the latest happenings in the colony. The latest, of course, was Linhares' return and sudden departure from Pamplona; and as always, Mrs. Leal seemed to have the details of the visit.

"For one thing, I made it a point to get to the bottom of the affair, and what better source than the *corno* of her husband?"

A few days later Mrs. Leal was again surrounded by her neighbors. She waited a few moments and then she said, "I must make it clear, I am not taking her husband's side; with me it is a matter of principle! As a true Portuguese, the matter of virtue is important; we must defend it."

The women drank the coffee in silence, waiting. She went on, "What I mean is, Linhares did not say he was the father of Ana's baby. This, from a man who is boastful about everything, proves that he is not. What do you think, neighbors?" The women nodded and she concluded, "We will have to call on our neighbor and do what must be done for the good of the colony. We will ask Ana to leave Pamplona as soon as possible."

"*Menina*," Mrs. Lucas said, "I don't think my husband would approve. Oh, I am not refusing; still, you see, my man keeps telling me I should mind my own business, keep house and help with the milking. As to other people's doings, you know how a man feels about things like the defense of virtue. A great foolishness, no less."

"That is why we women must be on guard. I, for one, won't stand for any *putedo* anywhere! We did something about it in the Old Country. Isn't our colony a true part of the land of our birth?" Mrs. Leal was quite emphatic about it.

Finally, after much discussion, a course of action was decided upon. The women would call at the Madruga ranch next Sunday, after lunch.

They thought it would be well to allow the old man enough time to eat, then present their demand.

Mrs. Costa felt that no harsh words should be spoken—only a demand in the simplest of terms. "After all," she explained, "we were all young once and the itching was common to all of us. The only thing was we feared the Devil, or perhaps the Devil was not up-to-date in his tricks to tempt us. We should be thankful for the strong and honest men we married, well able to take care of ourselves."

The women drank more coffee, so good and strong, then left, promising to return at the appointed time. "Don't fail me," Mrs. Leal warned. "We have a duty to perform. We've got to do it."

135

Roasting chicken was one of Ana's specialties. This one would be ready when they returned from Church. The way Madruga liked it was as tender as possible, moist, surrounded by potatoes, carrots, and in season, a piece or two of yellow squash. Of course, there was soup, containing the feet, wings, gizzard, and neck, thickened with a handful of rice, seasoned with herbs.

Eating at this hour in the peace of the day of rest, regardless of the two milkings, the old man liked to call Sunday that. He exclaimed with feelings that only Ana could prepare soup like that in California.

"Not only pretty, boy, but look at the gift you're getting. I tell you, you'll never go hungry."

Luis said nothing, proud of this girl who remained quiet, sitting as always near the old man. The recent visit by Linhares, and the details of what had happened, kept on coming to her in one phase or another, all the gruesome thoughts. So far, Luis had not been told. Perhaps some day it would be a proper thing to tell him. Her husband-to-be should take her knowing all that must be known. He must understand that fear of being hurt, her cowardice.

"How do you feel, girl?" These days Madruga showed great tenderness towards Ana. It was his respect for that child growing inside her, a child he hoped to see and hold in his arms before death came. Now, more than ever, he wanted to live. He must see Dr. Barboza and have him look him over again. He wanted to go on, a few more years at least. For one thing, he must make sure that Ana married Luis, and that the child would be fully recognized as his, if that was at all necessary.

"This last rain has been worth millions, boy. Our barley will come up and the new alfalfa. A few more showers later on, no frost; if that happens we'll be in good shape. We will have plenty of feed, make a few extra dollars, which, after all, is what I expect you to do if you buy half of the ranch. That's what you're planning to do, isn't it?"

Luis nodded. "Yes, Tio. Now I'll go into it without fear. We'll have someone to help us at the proper time. Isn't that right, Ana?" She did not reply.

"Well, then," Madruga said, "we better see Mr. Silveira again. Draw some kind of paper, but of course, we'll have to agree on the price, the rate of interest, payments; buying a ranch and buying a share in a dairy is about the same thing, isn't it? We could go tomorrow morning."

"Yes, Tio."

136

The knock at the front door was light, and apparently the people at the table did not hear it. As it grew louder, Ana said, "I think I hear someone at the door."

"Why, it's our neighbors," Madruga said. "Come in, Mrs. Leal. Yes, all of you come in."

"We can't stay too long," Mrs. Leal explained. "We didn't really come to visit. We want to have a word with Mrs. Linhares."

"Ana?" the old man said. "Yes, she is here. I'll call her."

The women came in shyly, following Mrs. Leal, a total of six. They were apologetic, regarding their number. "More were to come but at the last moment . . ."

"Girl," Madruga said, "our neighbors are here. They want to say something to you." Ana stood beside Tio and Luis.

"I was wondering," Mrs. Leal began, "couldn't we talk kind of private? Just us women."

"I have no secrets to hide either from Tio or Luis Sarmento." Ana's formality matched the stiffness in the manner of the women.

"We came," Mrs. Leal said, "as Portuguese from the Old Country, aware of our duties as members of the colony here in Pamplona. As such, and because of what you have done, we are asking you to leave. To us, the commission of adultery . . ." Mrs. Leal turned to her friends. "This is how we all feel, isn't it?"

In the silence that followed, she continued, "You know how we felt towards any errant female over there, and this big land hasn't changed us, not yet." With a certain air of finality she said, "When are you leaving, *senhora*?"

Madruga spoke up. "Ana is not going anywhere, but you are, here and now! Get out! I say, get out, all of you!" He was shaking a little as he spoke.

"We're only doing our duty, neighbor. A woman who deceives her husband, and we grant José Linhares was not one of the best, married by our Holy Church, can't escape certain obligations. These remain until death: every Christian woman knows that."

Mrs. Leal waited a moment. "We wouldn't be here now, except for one thing. I myself asked your husband if he was the father of the baby."

"You should have asked me," Luis said.

"Don't, *por favor*!" Ana said. "Let these *mexiriqueiras* alone! Let them burn in their own curiosity. Tio, can I ask them to go?"

"You can and I may say it before them—you're staying, unless you don't want to. You, my boy, there is work to do and you must do it, now that you're about to become owner of half of the ranch. You women should be ashamed of yourselves!"

"We're proud to do what we think is right. That's how we were brought up. America or not, we won't change."

"Go home, I say! Why, you look silly, standing in my house, accusing fingers and all!" His anger suddenly took over. "I say, get out!"

"We're going," Mrs. Leal said. "You may as well know it, neighbors or not, we don't intend to deal again with the shameless one."

Mrs. Leal walked haughtily down the stairs, then said to the other women, "We have done our duty and that's what counts, isn't it?" The little group walked away across the yard and out into the road.

"Where is my medicine?" Madruga asked Ana when they were alone again. "Why didn't I slap all of those *beatas*! They talk about *putas* and all that! Why, that Leal woman behaves like one!" Silently, Ana gave the old man his medicine.

"By the way," he said to Luis, "you better go and bring your cows in."

"Yes, Tio."

CHAPTER 14

Alone now, the old man said, "I must say you behaved very well, Ana. In the Old Country, I needn't tell you, there would be a lot more noise about matters like this. Yes, you were fine and so was Luis. He was a little afraid of himself, afraid of saying something he might be sorry for later. And it's good, I think. Luis will live to a ripe old age. A calm man. Aren't you glad of my forecast? Considering all things, I haven't done so bad myself. Past seventy, you see." Ana nodded. "I'll be a little selfish, if I may. I'd like to be here when the baby comes. That's right, Luis wants a boy."

"Yes, Tio, but you better take your medicine. Yesterday you forgot."

"I won't from now on."

"You should see the doctor again. How about tomorrow?"

"I will. Meanwhile, I want to warn you about what to expect from our neighbors. To their way of thinking, Ana, their visit to us means an end of their friendship. We are tainted, you see, because I offered you a home. Luis, they're sure, is the father of your child. And you are . . ."

"A *puta*. They are calling me that."

Madruga drank a glass of water slowly after taking his pill. "For one thing, you behave as you have. Let us not give our busybodies reasons to do more. You're both young and besides . . . you know, we'll have summer with us before we know it. Then your baby, it's not too long to wait, is it?" He got up from the table and said, "I think I'll go in and sleep a while, Ana."

"Thank God there aren't too many women like that around," Tio Corvello said a week or so later. "But the few living here can cause a lot of trouble, eh?"

Madruga nodded, sitting at the counter facing his friend.

"Why do they behave like that? The way I see it, they're against change. They still live as if they were in the Old Country. They speak Portuguese, eat Portuguese food, read Portuguese papers, listen to our radio programs. Change? How can they!"

Tio Madruga said, "Well, I did change. At least a little."

"You did, yes. Common sense did it, I suppose. Oh, I know it, you could have changed years ago; still, as the saying goes, it's better late than never."

They were silent a moment, and then Madruga spoke as if to himself. "It's not the harm they may do us; what hurts is we haven't done anything to anybody."

"I know," Corvello said. "How does Ana feel about this new form of cruelty, being ignored and all that? Has she talked of leaving again? But she won't, you can be sure. Isn't it wonderful to have a young woman around? Affection, that's all Ana has to offer and she gives you that with all her heart. I, too, wish I had someone. Too late, now."

Madruga nodded. A few dairymen were beginning to come in to buy their weekly supply of razor blades and tobacco. Seeing Madruga, they smiled, greeting him as in the old days, at least almost the same. There was a certain coolness, a certain hesitancy in their talk.

"I think I better go back," Madruga said finally.

"You may as well," Corvello said. "It must be very fine in your kitchen: there's that window and the fields all around. In no time everything will be tall alfalfa and grass on the ditch banks. You're very lucky."

The old man nodded. "Sometimes I sit alone, and I think of the years ahead, so few of them left. I think of the past, what has happened to me and what will happen when I am gone. The year 2000? I think of that, sometimes. An entire new cycle of time. But us, we'll be bones reduced to powder. Will the ranch be here then, still producing? The same trees?" He smiled. "This is senseless talk. It must be my age," he said, getting up.

"I don't know what it is, doctor. I quit the hard work. Just help around the kitchen, feed the calves once in a while. I sleep and take the stuff you prescribed. What I want to say, I feel tired all the time. My legs carry me with difficulty. This condition lasts a few days, maybe a week, and then I feel better. What causes it?"

"Your age, and other things. Worry, for instance. I suppose you've been hearing a lot about the girl. Her name is in every mouth."

"Yes."

"The gossips of Pamplona, those old women who still live in the narrow-mindedness of their villages in the islands of home, they'd rather have a girl commit an abortion and stay pure for the sake of a husband, who, I understand, is some sort of a queer bastard. The fact that a girl is healthy and attractive should be no excuse for normal behavior; you've got to obey the rules of marriage and wait for a better break in heaven."

Madruga smiled. He continued, "Running, or attempting to run a girl out of town, eh? I have news for you: here in America we still have native folks who behave like Mrs. Leal and her friends. Their approach is almost the same; harsh words are spoken, scandal is carried from household to household; and the errant female does occasionally leave town to see the abortionist; or, if this is too late, to some far city to give birth to a child left with someone and never to be seen again. All this is done for the sake of virtue and propriety."

Dr. Barboza smiled, evidently enjoying his own speech. "As for your trouble, the way I see it, your heart is slowing down. Your heart may stop. You understand?" Madruga nodded. "No overexertion. Sit, don't overeat. Remember your first warning last year."

"How can I remain cool? So much is happening around me. That baby—I want to be here when it comes."

"You will. You're a good patient. I'm sure you will do as I ask."

"Yes, I'm calling at the drugstore to order your medicine."

"Shouldn't Ana be coming in? She's due for another visit."

The beauty of spring exploded all over the valley. The rains had been plentiful at the right time. The weeks of fog preceding the final clearing of the sky kept the moisture in the soil; new grass covered the sides of the roads; wild flowers carpeted the hills in blue and yellow.

The excitement of the new season was felt by everyone. Plans made in the winter were put into effect; the men watched the land and judged the quantity of future returns; how many tons of hay, how many sacks of barley per acre, how many bales of cotton. Sitting in his usual chair on the porch, Tio Madruga pondered many things, but enthusiasm was not present. He recalled Barboza's advice.

The past of long ago came back in great detail: the porch was now the deck of a whaling ship; around him was the sea, a wide circle of moving blue water. He was a sailor again, a real *baleeiro*—his eyes keen on any sounding, calling for that shrill cry which every whaleman knows by heart. The dream continued: Madruga saw many islands peopled by lovely women, where one could find food and sweet water.

He could hear again the great discussions, where ambergris could be found and more important, gold itself, in the mountains of California. "That's how I came here," the old man thought. "I did not find much gold, but I have found this land needing a lot of care and water."

"It hadn't been too bad," Madruga thought, as he continued to live in the past. "The land was cheap, almost flat and the climate mild; it was never too cold in the winter months; and in the summer the breeze from the sea always came over the mountains to cool the valley." "Why must one age so soon," the old man wondered. Here he was, afraid to move, truly a coward, remembering the doctor's warnings, yet there was so much work to do and he alone to do it. He got up slowly and went to his room to change.

"I'm going to see the Portuguese lawyer this morning, another talk, I guess, and when I come back I'll see Luis," he told Ana.

"He's in the field, Tio," Ana said. She was big already, carried herself well and, one suspected, with a certain pride.

"I know where he is," Madruga said. "I'd be there myself except for that fool doctor's advice. All this because a man tires a little! Don't tell me Barboza is not tired himself, seeing people the way he does all day." Ana nodded, smiling. "But to me he says, 'Cut out the foolishness, slow up or you'll die.' He's a damn fool, that man!"

"It's about time I came to pay my respects," Father Ribeiro, the new priest in Pamplona, said, walking in at Ana's invitation. He stood uneasily in the center of the living room, looking toward the kitchen. "This is no hour to visit anyone, really, but I may as well be truthful: I was hoping you'd be about to serve something remindful of the food of our islands; and, as the Lord will have it, I think you were about to serve kale soup for lunch! If so, may I be asked to join you in eating a bowl of it?"

"Yes, there's enough for all of us," Ana said. "Come in. I want you to meet Luis Sarmento and Mr. Aguiar. Tio Madruga, the owner of the ranch, should be here soon. He knew, before he left, that his special food was being cooked."

"After so many years, does he still think of the food of home? I understand he has been here half a century."

The priest watched the green soup being ladled into his bowl. "Isn't that wonderful!" he began. "We at the parish house eat well; there is meat on the table and all that, but something like this! Let it be called the food of the poor; it doesn't matter, a taste of the many things we find here, to fully appreciate what we left." Smiling, Father Ribeiro asked, "How long have you been in America, *filha*?"

"A little over a year," Ana replied.

"Tell me, do you like this country?"

As Ana did not answer at once, "Oh, I know. In the beginning one does get lost, eh?" Quickly he added, "But I must say, I am not an expert in these matters: I've only been here a short time."

"All I can say is," Mr. Aguiar said, "I came to California to earn a few dollars. My wife is waiting for me over there, and I plan to leave as soon as I can. If you work hard you really have no time to think of anything. The food is good here and there's plenty of it. You eat your fill and do your chores. What more could one want?"

"Peace of mind, I guess," the priest said. "Now, take Mrs. Linhares, a young woman, married, who I understand, has been abandoned by her husband. Peace of mind is very important to her now. There is this child coming, *filha*. I must tell you, I have been informed of your coming motherhood."

There was silence in the room and Ana said, "That means you already know the details. The women of Pamplona!"

"If you'll excuse me," Aguiar said, "I think I'll go to my room and sleep a little. Goodbye, Father."

Ana waited a few moments. "What I want to say is that my child was conceived out of wedlock, my husband was a *maricas*. You've been told all this, haven't you?" The priest waited. "I want you to meet the father of my baby, Luis."

The dark, well-featured face of the priest turned to young Sarmento.

Ana continued. "It was he who understood and comforted me. Here on this ranch I found love for the first time: that something the women of our colony call mortal sin."

The priest's gaze left Luis, still silent, for a moment. "What you did, wasn't it a mortal sin? To commit adultery—surely the power of love must not supercede suffering? You had no excuse, Ana Linhares." The priest paused a moment. "Another half bowl of soup, *por favor*."

Eating it slowly, relishing each mouthful, he said, "But you are a good cook, *senhora*. Why your husband left you, a healthy young woman not neglected in good looks by God!" Father Ribeiro blushed a little, then turning to Luis, he asked, "Now you tell me your side of the story."

Luis smiled. "In the confessional, Father, only there."

"A good idea. I may as well say it, I came here not only to meet you, the women of the colony suggested . . ."

"You are not joining them Father! We have been asked to leave."

"That is how we did it back there, isn't it?" the priest said. "But personally, sinners can become saints, and who are we to condemn the helpless young?"

Ana and Luis sat listening in silence to this man from the Azores, who, they were sure, understood their problem.

"I would at once apply to our ecclesiastical office for an annulment of the marriage. But, I must warn you, Our Holy Mother frowns on the dissolution of what was meant to be forever. Anyway, you come to the parish house tomorrow. Are you in full agreement, young man?"

"Yes, sir."

"Oh, by the way, I celebrate Mass at nine-thirty next Sunday." Getting up, ready to leave, "Whenever you cook something like this, I'll be happy to come and have lunch with you, *senhora*. Anytime!"

"I'd buy this tract, if I were you," Madruga said to Luis. They were in the center of the ranch leaning against the barbed wire fence. "What I mean is, I had the land surveyed years ago and the center of this lane, either side, is sixty acres. As to the buildings, there's the house on one side and the barn and tankhouse on the other. By choosing the barn, as you already sleep in the tankhouse . . ." the old man smiled, "in the old days wherever you slept didn't matter too much, the barn was always the important building. Your cows were milked and you kept your food there."

Madruga continued, "Buying a ranch is an immigrant's final step in America. A piece of ground you like to call home. Do you like Pamplona well enough to want to stay?"

Luis smiled. "Our people asked us to leave, Tio."

"It's true," the old man agreed. "It will take a little time for their anger to pass."

Luis nodded. "Tio, I want to live here. I'll buy the tract you suggest."

"Good!" the old man said. "Now for the price: I'll treat you as a stranger. I don't want folks to say I'm giving you special consideration. The interest will be five percent a year on the unpaid balance. I'll give you twenty years to pay. The price is to be five hundred an acre. It's a fair price, I think. Will you be able to pay thirty thousand dollars, interest and taxes, in twenty years?"

"I think so, Tio."

"You'll be young yet, and I won't be here, but someone will be here to collect." Luis nodded. "What is important is that I have paid for all I have by hard work. You'll do the same."

"I will."

"Hard work and love, you've got to love this land; attend to its needs, irrigate it at the right time; harvest the crops; manure it; and when your son is old enough, you must teach him what you know. Start him early; give him a calf; have him attend to it all by himself. A growing heifer calf. Is there a better project for a growing boy? Of course, you'll be talking a lot, telling him how to do things; maybe a ride on the tractor when the alfalfa reaches up to your knee, and it's not too hot, and the sky is all blue up there.

"Do you think this is a fair price, payments, interest, everything?"

"Yes, Tio."

"And how much money have you for a down payment? It's the custom in America, boy."

"Twelve hundred dollars. Is that enough?"

"Yes," said the old man. "For both of us. You see, now that you're about to become a father, I'll just take five hundred to close the deal." Luis waited. "Well, then, I'll see our lawyer in the morning and have him write up the contract."

145

"Yes," Luis said adding, "Thank you."

The old man became startled at this. "Thank me for what? Because I sold you half of this ranch? Do you know how many milkings it will take to pay for it, how many cold, wet mornings, how many trips to the creamery? How many evenings watching a sick animal, the plowing, the sowing and the harvesting? But I know you'll do all this and pay every dollar."

Now the two were silent as they walked toward the buildings, clean white and red, under the morning sun.

On Sunday, Father Ribeiro delivered his sermon in a typical Portuguese fashion. His arms moved about with great gestures, his long, brown fingers pointing in various directions—mostly towards Mrs. Leal, some of the parishioners said—and his voice, strong and clear, seemed to shake the walls of the Church.

"In this big land," the priest began, "living among strange people, away from the beloved sounds that one knew, the foods of home, oh, so many things, one is bound to be tempted into sin; and temptation assumes many forms. To our young, suddenly transplanted to a wonderful country of bread and meat, sweets, and sweet music, a land where all things are possible, the stern rules of morality may be forgotten. The present, only the present, is important. What matters is any act that may fulfill the emptiness, be it drink or fornication."

The priest paused and now his voice was calm. "But I, a priest of God, will not condemn the guilty without a full examination of what caused their fall." He became specific by degrees. "I will now return to your daily lives: the emptiness, and the eventual desire to sin. I'll take as an example any young Portuguese woman recently come from the Azores. This woman is alone, or perhaps she is not; either way, she is dazzled with the greatness, the beauty, the excitement; at once, temptation walks by her side. If you're alone, tears are in themselves conducive to sin. When the heart hurts, any touch of the hand—we, the older, who claim to sit at the Lord's table, what do we do? We refuse to understand. We pass blind judgment. We follow the narrow road of tradition. We become judges and executioners. This is not the way of Christ. He, who consorted with publicans, who let the Magdalen anoint His feet—we, the small bits of Portugal scattered all over California and the eastern states, must try to understand each other. Let the love of God cement us in full comprehension of the problems ahead, give us courage to fulfill our obligations to the land of our adoption, loving it with respect, yet conscious of our own glorious past."

The priest made the sign of the cross above his congregation, then returned to the altar.

"He was talking for our benefit," Mrs. Costa said later.

Mrs. Leal agreed. "I suppose we deserve it; still, I believe we did what was right as Christian women. And we weren't too hard on Ana."

"We should go back and apologize," Mrs. Lucas suggested.

"When the baby comes, we'll have a chance to see it, bring something along, a small gift; it doesn't take much to right things, the way I see it." The women nodded, walking to their cars. Sunday or not, there were the usual chores waiting in their kitchens.

147

"The time is here for our annual race, boy," Tio Madruga said one day at sunrise, "but I won't be out there this year." Recalling the past, he continued, "It was good in the old days. There were no tractors around, just horses and mules. I had the biggest team of bay horses in Pamplona, well trained, gentle as babies. You walked behind them, raking the hay; you had to know your way in the dark. Ah, that breeze on your face! You felt wonderful then. The work was nothing." The old man waited a moment. "I'd really give anything to be out there again!"

"You stay with Ana, Tio. If she will let you, help her with the breakfast."

"I will cook breakfast," he said.

Luis nodded. "I better be going, Tio. If Ana wants anything . . ."

"Ana will be all right," he said. "When her time comes I'll drive her to Barboza's hospital myself. She is going to have her son in the American way, a doctor, nurses, everything: a fine room; her food will be brought to her; good-tasting things. They say when you have babies you should eat the best, chicken—they used to serve that to all mothers on the islands."

Luis smiled. "You should really go back to bed, Tio. It's still too early."

"No, no, boy! I'll walk down to the yard. Aguiar will soon be up. I'll watch him milk."

"No lifting of anything heavy, remember."

"I won't, boy."

Alone in the yard, Madruga felt the loose gravel under his feet as he walked. This was a nice clean place since the boy's arrival from the Old Country. He remembered the tall weeds, the twisted planks and rubbish. Luis had changed all that. Why, that boy had begun on the very first day of his arrival, still tired from the voyage! That's what happens when you are young and ambitious. Luis had always been that way: a hard worker, willing to learn; a quiet one; a plodder. Madruga smiled. Well, one had to be in the beginning: spend months away from everybody; no shaving, unless you did it yourself. Bathing? When you could. No wonder it was always an event, that trip to town twice a month.

Well, it was different now. The houses were better, warmer, no kerosene lights—butane or electricity took its place at reasonable prices. Yes, things had changed with the years, but not completely in his case. He thought of the kitchen where, notwithstanding its modernity, the old wood stove still held its position of importance: cottonwood, yes, dry cottonwood, smelling of the fields, would always warm it insofar as he was concerned. Then he thought of the woodpile, cut to size, dwindling away, a chore he did every year. "Summer or not, I could just as well cut a few branches while I can." One never knew: there could be a hard winter to contend with and now with the small one coming . . .

Mr. Aguiar walked down, greeting Madruga in his usual manner. "Another nice day," he said. Then he walked to the faucet and opened it, submerged his face in the tub, snorting like a seal. Then he said, "I better go out and bring them in."

"Luis did it already," the old man said. "See our cows coming our way?"

Aguiar nodded. "I should have known. That boy thinks of everything."

"He does," Madruga said. "That's why I sold him half of the ranch yesterday."

"You couldn't have found a better young man," Aguiar said. "I know, I've been working with him. He's a born dairyman. He'll amount to something one day."

"He must," Madruga had followed Aguiar to the barn. "I want him to be a man of responsibility, do what most Americans do. He must belong, go ahead in the American way. Think of this land as his land; he must do that. That has been the trouble with us in the past: we bought land, but improvements—we didn't have the money needed for a lot of things. We planted, cut grass, milked our animals by hand. Anybody who came and tried to show us new methods, ordinary things like milking machines, we simply would not listen." Madruga waited, watching the line of cows eating the newly-cut alfalfa.

"Luis Sarmento began to learn the new ways as soon as he arrived on the ranch and he could see a good thing at once. You didn't have to spend an hour explaining what to do or not to. Before long he was explaining things to me! That is why I decided to modernize our ranch. Oh, you should have seen this place before he came!" Aguiar said nothing. "Anyway, I had the money to improve things. There it was, in the bank earning interest; interest meant more money, and after a while I wanted to do something with it."

It was daylight now. Trucks began to drive away from the farms noisily on their way to the creameries in town. A Southern Pacific train left Pamplona, its bell clanging mournfully in the silence of the new morning.

"I better go and fix breakfast," Madruga said as he left.

Ana was already in the kitchen preparing the usual breakfast of sausage and eggs and beans. Mr. Aguiar ate a large bowlful every morning. "Can't do without them," he used to say. "You've got to get something inside your belly, to give you a push with the work."

"Why didn't you stay in bed a while longer?" Madruga asked. "I believe I can cook breakfast without causing Barboza undue worry. Besides, I don't have to tell him what I do from day-to-day."

"You should," Ana said. "You owe it to yourself to be careful."

"Girl," the old man said, "if I was to obey that man, do everything he asks me to do, I'd end up twenty-four hours a day in bed! I'm not going to stand for this foolishness. Besides, I've never felt better in my life."

Ana smiled. "I'll let you set the table, just that." Her near-motherhood was quite evident now. She was large, moved about slowly; her face remained calm, reflecting peace within. Without being told, she somehow knew she had been forgiven by the colony. She saw no hatred or disdain in her neighbors' behavior toward her. Now she wondered what it would be like, giving birth to a dear, live being, who would cling to her, depend on her for everything. What would her reaction be after the pain of delivery?

"How many more weeks, girl?" Madruga asked, as if he had joined Ana in her worry. "When is the baby due?"

"Dr. Barboza says, in a matter of six weeks or so."

"I see," said the old man, placing the plates on the table. Then he walked to the window and looked out. "The sun is up. Aguiar should be almost done. Luis—yes I see him on the lane walking back. He's always on time to eat."

"Now, will you please sit?" Madruga said. "From now on, old Tomé will be in charge of things, Barboza's orders or not. You won't cook, do the beds. Can you imagine, in six weeks or less!" It was as if the full impact of Ana's time of delivery had just then been understood by the old man.

"Tio, please—why, my mother, the women in the Azores worked until the first birth pains came."

"It's different here, *filha*. In America, it's different. You'll see."

Luis walked in, followed by Aguiar. "Oh, what a fine crop, Tio," Luis said. "Up to here," he pointed to his waist. "Thick, too. At least three bales per acre!" Suddenly he saw Ana. "How do you feel?"

The girl smiled. "Wonderful, and now that Tio is going to be in charge of the kitchen, you see, I mustn't lift even a finger until the baby comes."

"Don't you think it's a good idea? You should take it easy, really."

"Yes," Ana said, impatiently. "I'll let you know when I need help. But for the present, no."

"Why, I can help," Mr. Aguiar offered. "All of us will."

"By the way," Madruga said to the milker, "wait for me a bit. I want to go to town with you."

"Yes, Tio," Mr. Aguiar said.

The old man was Penney's first customer that morning. Mrs. Vieira guessed his apprehension at once, as he walked into the still-empty store.

"Good morning, Tio. You're early. What may I show you?"

He was very direct. "I'm about to become a grandfather, *senhora*, and I'd like to buy those things necessary, a present for the young people who live on my ranch."

"Luis and the girl? I have heard about them. I want to tell you, you are a good man, keeping them with you in spite of what they say. You need good friends when you're in trouble. You were right there all along."

"Thank you," Madruga said politely. "I guess you know we don't care what anyone says as long as we do the best we can. This reminds me— you've had children of your own, yes? I mean, you might help me," smiling. "I'm really too old to be a grandfather; still, I may as well tell you, I've had the grandest time ever since those two arrived on my ranch. They laugh and talk about the future and all that is wonderful to hear."

Mrs. Vieira nodded understandingly. "Yes," she said, "now, as to what you want, we should begin with a crib."

"Ah, yes, that." Suddenly he remembered the cribs fashioned of rum casks in the savage islands of the Pacific, and his own crib, patiently carved by his father out of a cedar trunk.

"Come along, Tio, we'll show you what we have." The old man followed the saleslady to a back room of the store, a dream room decorated in pink and blue, displaying life-sized storks standing in the center of a long display table. The various counters were stocked high with merchandise; soft music played from an unseen loudspeaker.

"This one is nice," Mrs. Vieira said. "Of course, we can give you one in pink or blue, according to the baby's sex. We should follow the custom."

"It's going to be a boy," Madruga said calmly.

Mrs. Vieira smiled. "It will have to be. It's a natural thing to have a boy by your side in the beginning. The land—it takes a man to work it. A boy, yes. I hope your wishes will come true," Mrs. Vieira said. "Understand, there must be girls also. Later."

153

"I want one I can rock with my foot, the way we used to do it in the Old Country."

"Those young years in your island, you still think of them, don't you?"

"Yes," the old man agreed. "Now everything comes back. Very clear. Things like the feel of water on my legs when I used to wade across Ribeira Grande, or the squirm of an eel wrapped around my wrist. But I came here to buy a few things for my grandson. A crib, oh, yes. This one will be fine."

"Baby clothes. Diapers first, naturally."

"Whatever is needed. You know all about those things."

"Yes."

"I'll give you a check as soon as I come back from the barber. Hold everything here in the store until I call for it later." The old man walked out of the store in his usual sure step.

"I better go back," Luis said to Ana. "I've got to finish the field."

"We should hire a relief milker," Ana said. "All this work, it's too much for you and Mr. Aguiar."

"No, Ana. Am I to become soft in the beginning? We have an indebtedness to discharge to Tio, or his estate; and it will be discharged, I promise you. I must show everyone. No favors, you see. Whatever I own, it will be paid in full by our own work. It's the custom, as Tio would say."

Ana smiled, taking his hands in hers. "Are you coming back for lunch?"

Luis shook his head. "Leave something on the stove."

"I will."

"Be careful. Lock the door."

Ana pondered Luis's apprehension. Without saying so, it was his fear of Linhares' return. But he would not, Ana thought. What he had done—the vengeance implied his need had been fulfilled. Indeed, he had paid her back. To José, it had been enough. Yet she locked herself in and returned to the kitchen.

Now she began to think of what she must buy to clothe her baby. She must go to Pamplona soon, to get ready. In the Azores, a woman was helped by her neighbors. They came in, visited a little, advised, retold the story of their own deliveries, sewing little garments, meanwhile. Of course, the midwife came in too, wise in her ways, sharp in her comments. But here she was in America, cooking, keeping house alone.

Suddenly she recalled Father Ribeiro's visit a few days before. "I have seen the bishop and he assures me your marriage can be annulled. One thing, though, and of this you must be continually aware, it will take time. The Church is always slow in these matters, even though your case seems to be a clear one." Ana remembered the priest's smile as he concluded, "Of course, there is the matter of the baby, we must think of that."

Time, Ana agreed in silence, time to do all these things. She sat by the window without seeing anything in particular.

At midnight weeks later, Madruga was awakened by Ana's cries, soft, not too loud, as if she did not want to disturb anyone. The old man listened attentively, his head lifted from his pillow, resting on the palm of one hand. Surely, he thought. He bounded out of bed and rushed to the telephone. He suddenly paused—he must consult Ana, find out what was bothering her. "Girl?"

"Yes, Tio."

"What is the matter, *rapariga*?"

"A pain. A very sharp pain a minute ago. It's gone now."

"I'll call Barboza."

"It's nothing, maybe . . ."

But Madruga did not hear, he was already calling the doctor on the telephone—"Yes, a sharp pain. Comes and goes."

The old man waited, listening. "Yes, I'll bring her over. We'll be in your office as soon as I'm dressed."

Then he called Luis. "It's time, boy. The doctor is waiting. Come down and start the truck."

They drove to Pamplona over the country road in the dark. "Be careful, watch out for bumps."

"I'm being careful," Luis said. "Ana, you'll be all right. It's nothing. Besides, Barboza is a good man."

"You stay with me, and you, Tio."

In the hospital finally, the nurse made Ana ready. "The doctor will be here in a few minutes. He's drinking some coffee. You two go back to the waiting room."

"Did you tell Mr. Aguiar about it? The cows have to be milked."

"I did, boy. He knows what to do." Luis nodded. "You're not worried, are you? As the father, I'm told . . ."

"Oh, no," Luis said, "Ana will come out all right."

He hoped so; he had been responsible for her condition, and he alone. He should have fought his helpless love, recognized sin and abstained from it. Ah, Ana had been so helpless. Well, now the harm had been done, and the next move was marriage, as soon as possible. He must give a name to his child, assure it and his mother of a decent living. Of this he was certain: Tio had taught him everything—how to be frugal, to work hard, when to buy and sell, to save, to respect the past and plan for the future.

The old man startled Luis. "I wonder how long it will take?"

Luis shrugged his shoulders, preferring to be silent.

"In the savage islands," the old man began, "the chore of having children was an easy one. I recall an instance. I was a young whaler then and saw a native girl giving birth. Unseen, I was at a little distance from her. She was under a tree, squatting and crying now and then. Soon it came: she dropped the child and wrapped it in a piece of cloth and walked away." The old man smiled. "It's better the way it's done in America."

"Yes, Tio."

"It costs a little money—doctor and the hospital—but you're helped, and they tell me it's a painful mess, to say the least. Barboza is a good man at these things, I'm told."

"Suppose it's a girl?" Madruga said. "It could be." This was his first

155

admission of doubt. To think that Ana's first might be a girl! Indeed, he had been too sure before.

"It won't matter, Tio," Luis said. It was daylight now. The first pickups drove by on their way to the creamery. From the fields nearby came the muffled sound of tractors. A boy on a bike raced down Pacheco Avenue.

The bell at Saint Joseph's called the faithful to early Mass. Meanwhile, the old man slept, his back on the chair, the long legs extended. "He should have stayed at home," Luis thought. There was no necessity; sure, he could have asked him to stay, but there was no stopping him in what he wanted to do. He obeyed no one: Dr. Barboza, Ana, Corvello. Oh, he took his medicine, rested more, and all that, but a change in his behavior and habits was not accomplished.

Mrs. Barboza, the doctor's wife, in charge of the hospital, walked noiselessly into the reception room. She was a lovely woman, gray-haired, possessing a young, mobile, and at times sad face. She smiled, seeing the old man asleep.

In a low voice she spoke to Luis. "You're the father of a fine boy. Congratulations. Should I wake Mr. Madruga? I think we had better tell him."

She placed a hand on the sleeping man's shoulder. "Ana has a present for you, Tio. Come along."

They entered a small, white room. Ana lay in bed, her child asleep on her arm. "You have a grandson, Tio."

The old man kissed her on her forehead. Then, with his small finger, he touched ever-so-slightly the baby's little hand. "Thank you, *filha*," he said.

Watching Luis holding Ana's hand, he asked, "How do you feel? The boy—is he all right?"

"Of course he is," said the doctor, walking in. "Now will you two get out? Let this girl sleep."

In the corridor Barboza caught up with Madruga.

"How is the old pump working these days?"

"Oh, fine," the old man said. "Why, I'd like to run as fast as a calf this morning. All the way to the ranch—I've never felt so good!"

CHAPTER 16

The women returned to Madruga's house one Sunday afternoon a few days after Ana came back from the hospital. They brought gifts, a few items of clothing for the child.

The reason for this visit had been prearranged through their husbands, in a more-or-less casual way. The men approached Madruga, waited for his reactions, and these in turn were passed on to the women.

"My door is always open to anyone who wishes to come in with good intentions. What has taken place is past. We have no bitterness."

It was about two in the afternoon when the ladies walked into the yard. "Let us be as natural as possible, neighbors. It's the proper thing to do."

They walked up slowly and entered the screened porch. Mrs. Leal knocked, a medium, friendly knock.

"Why, hello," Madruga said, opening the door. He turned to Ana and Luis, "Come here, you two. We have callers."

The young couple entered the living room. "We were watching our baby. He's sleeping now."

Mrs. Leal could become quite sentimental at times. "After what we did and said, yes, we had to come and say we know better now. We should have known this is a new land. Things are done differently here. Besides, your husband, God forgive him for what he did—anyway, we came back and brought a few things for the little one. For you, too, Ana. I remember you used to like my sweet bread. Here's a loaf, baked only yesterday."

"We can't say more than Mrs. Leal has said. Oh, it's all true. We should have known better. We were such stupid women!"

"Busybodies—that's what we were," Mrs. Costa said.

"Indeed," Mrs. Lucas agreed.

"Will you make some coffee, Luis?" said Ana. "Would you like to see the baby?"

"Oh yes," Mrs. Ferreira said.

"We really came for that," Mrs. Lucas said truthfully.

They marched, single file into the kitchen. "How lovely," Mrs. Leal said. "How lovely to be young and the mother of a treasure like that."

"Oh, yes," the others said, bending around the crib, watching the sleeping child in silence for a few moments.

"I'll set the table," Luis said. As he did so Mrs. Lucas said, "God will bless you; you made a lonely woman happy, boy. We know now what kind of a pig her husband was. Phew!"

"Thank you, Tia."

They sat around the table, drank coffee and ate Mrs. Leal's bread. She said, "I'll go back and get another loaf. Imagine, me eating my own present!"

"Tomorrow. That will be time enough," Ana said. "I'm glad you've come. We admit it—what we did was wrong."

"I know," Mrs. Leal answered promptly. "We all know."

"We won't talk about it anymore. The important thing is that I am a grandfather and have a son and a daughter," Mr. Madruga said. "Why, I'm not alone anymore."

"How true, Tio," the women said together.

They left laughing and talking. "We'll come again, Ana, and whenever you need anything, we're a big Portuguese family in America, aren't we?"

Luis wanted to laugh. "Thank you, neighbors," he said.

"About our little remembrances for the baby, if you want to exchange anything, see Mrs. Vieira at Penney's."

At the gate on their way out, Mrs. Leal had the last word. "If only they could marry in our Church, but it's too much to hope for."

Mr. Garcia's annual visit to Pamplona—the Pentecost Feast was quite early this year—and his store of news from all over California, brought ease to Mrs. Leal's misgivings about a civil marriage, and more directly the solution of Ana Linhares' immediate problem.

He arrived at Corvello's early one morning, stored his sample cases in the back room and walked to the counter.

"It's worth it, coming all the way from Sacramento. Suits you can always sell, but these beans! Do you know, my wife doesn't know how to fix them the way you do? I just don't know what it is—maybe it's the seasoning."

"Or the pot," Corvello explained. "The pot does it, I think. Now, in the Old Country, that's the way we did it. We had no white bread to eat with them, though. Corn bread, and that was good. Of course, sometimes we didn't have enough."

Tio Corvello said, "What is new in suits this year?"

"Better material, for one thing. New stripes and squares, new colors. Blues, greens, and browns." With his mouth full, he continued, "I have added a new department to my business: after today I'll be taking orders for wedding suits, the best blue or black material you ever saw."

159

"Count me out on that one," Corvello said, laughing.

"Wherever I go," Garcia said, "there will always be some young man in love. Love means marriage; and that means I'll be doing business all over California, summer and winter. Isn't that a fine idea?"

"I think it is," Corvello agreed. "But will you still have time to come and visit us?"

"Oh yes," he said as he finished his meal. "How is de Castro these days?"

"The same. A new girl every week for our young. Room, a girl, and a shave—or maybe it's the other way around. Anyway, he makes a living."

"No doubt about it," Garcia agreed. "Everybody needs a haircut now and then. Anyway, I do now. Tomorrow I'll visit the ranches. A clean look and a smile, that's the secret of success!"

"Talk, you can do a lot of that," Tio Corvello said laughing.

Garcia walked into Madruga's kitchen early the next day. Mr. Aguiar was still eating and Luis stood nearby drinking coffee.

"He's early this year, isn't he?" Madruga said, and followed the salesman into the kitchen.

"The day of the celebration dictates my time, you should know. When you have the state of California as your territory . . . How is everybody?" he asked sitting down.

"Fine," the old man answered. "I've never felt so good in my life, except for the shortness of breath when I do anything. By the way, what's new in suits this year?"

"I will not answer that, old man. I sold you a *roupa* last year, didn't I? A fine black one, suited to any occasion. I bet you wore it only once. There would be no need of another. I don't believe in overloading people. That is not the way. But boy, you do need a good suit."

"I may not even go to the celebration," Luis demurred.

"All Portuguese must go to the celebration, *rapaz*." Being Spanish, Garcia's accent on the word did not sound just right. "I may as well show you a few samples."

Ana had cleared the table and the salesman opened his sample case and proceeded in silence to turn the various cardboard squares over, one by one. Then he paused. "This one, boy, feel it. Light as a feather."

"How much?" Luis asked.

"Reasonable enough, considering the various uses you could make out of it. For one, the celebration." With a mischievous smile on his face, he said, "Did you know I also take orders for wedding suits?"

He turned to Ana. "Oh, by the way, I have news for you, Mrs. Linhares." Garcia's face was now devoid of mirth. "About your husband, I mean. I don't think you know about it, not yet. It happened a week ago, near Eureka."

"My husband's place of work. I didn't know."

Garcia nodded. "You see, he didn't stay in San Diego. The fishing, remember? It was hard, he said, and it meant months at sea away from everybody. He didn't want that. That's what they told me down there he said. So he traveled all the way up to Eureka. A few days here, a week there. Just enough time to earn a dollar to eat. Always moving, the Linhares way. No more milking for him, he told me last spring. The woods were the place where one could work and earn thousands in a short while. Cut a tree, and there's always another; there's food, all you want to eat; and you can get drunk if you want to and find a girl."

Garcia emptied his cup and said, "By the way, I know what took place between you and your man. It's a part of my business to listen to a little gossip and pass it on."

"So Linhares is working in a lumber mill," Ana said. "He used to talk to me about forests, even in the Azores."

Garcia said, "I wouldn't have mentioned your husband's name but I received a letter from a bartender friend just a few days ago. He wrote to say Linhares is dead."

Silence ensued around the table for a few moments. "That bragging, loud-mouthed man is gone!" Madruga said. "May God have pity on him."

"Yes," Ana said.

"He was drunk for a week, I was told, refused food, and they said he fell out of bed on the cement floor and injured his head."

"At least a Mass for his soul," Madruga said, after a pause. "I'll see the priest about it tomorrow."

He said to Garcia, "You may as well go on and call on our colony. Then, when you're done, come back and see Luis. Two suits. I'm sure he'll buy two."

"I'll be back in two or three days," Garcia said.

161

It was good to be at home in full charge of the baby. He had been shown how to feed it, how to hold it in his arms. He liked to do that, sitting by the kitchen window, watching the ranch outside. There was that exquisite pleasure of rocking it to sleep. The baby's small cries and that incomprehensible small talk were sweet music to hear. Really, the baby should be in Ana's room, yet by common preference the crib was always in the kitchen.

"It's sunny for one thing. Besides, the appliances are new and white, except for the old wood stove."

"It's all right, Tio."

"It has to be. What would we do if we didn't have a place to burn our dry cottonwood; we have so much."

Madruga smiled, recalling the conversation a few days before. "Come to think of it, I should really saw a few chunks at a time— shouldn't be too much of a job."

Indeed, these were special days when Luis and Ana drove to Pamplona. Then, all by himself he could take a general inventory of his life, and the aftermath was always a pleasant one. Yes, it had taken faith and a lot of work: loneliness in the beginning. But it passed; after a while he quit thinking about it. He had his time to the full, time for payments, marketing, cultivating, and finally after decades, Luis and Ana.

Now his plans were complete. Linhares' death had somehow given them solidity. The two young ones could marry, become a respectable couple in the colony. As to the land, cattle and equipment, Madruga stopped rocking the crib. The child was asleep.

He walked to the cold wood stove and put his hands on it. How old it was! He had purchased it during that terrible flu epidemic to keep the house warm. A long time ago.

In the safety of the crib, the baby would sleep at least an hour, long before his parents would return. He might as well walk outside. A light breeze met his face. This was one of those lovely days of summer, tempting, as it were, all persons to go into some form of activity.

Madruga felt this invisible pull, a strange craving to do something, regardless of his doctor's advice. Of course! He would walk a little. Exercise. Not too much of it. Why not feed the calves? Surely this would not be too exhaustive a chore.

After a while he walked aimlessly to the wood pile. The dry cottonwood branches were there. At least a few. Why not? He sat on an empty tomato crate in order to be as comfortable as possible.

Surely Barboza would approve of this, no chore at all. The wood was soft; the saw made a soft, relaxing sound. After a while, reality seemed to be passing away from him . . . the saw handle was now the handle of an oar . . . he was at sea again . . . in a light whaling boat . . . as he pulled and pulled he thought he saw a great whale . . . far, waiting out there. He must cut the seas fast, get to his prize ahead of anyone; there was no time to lose, no time.

Now something of great importance was happening, the big monster . . . the boat itself, was fading away, covered by a thick gray fog. Sounds about him became mute, small, like a breeze suddenly becoming still. The pause had finally touched him and there was no end to it.

Ana and Luis found Tomé Madruga a short time later still holding the saw handle in his hand, his face against a cottonwood branch.

They came to the pool hall after the funeral to drink a glass of wine or beer, quite uncomfortable in their tight, serge suits. Corvello sat on his usual stool at the end of the counter. A Portuguese newspaper lay unfolded before him, as he talked between sips of black coffee. His words could be construed as a kind of eulogy on the passing of Tomé Madruga.

"He was a Portuguese who made good in America, the way I see it.

Came here without a penny, just a wish to work and make his home in this big land. Like all of us, he had to pay his passage fare and now and then send a few dollars to his parents."

Mr. Corvello swatted a fly, gorging itself on a drop of wine and continued, "While some of us are still trying, still hoping to be somebody, Madruga died already somebody, owner of land and cattle, a happy man, hearing laughter around him—a man who held in his hand a young boy, a boy, who, for all we know, will be remembered by him. It's true, these pleasures came to him quite late in life; still, he was able to savor what we have never known and perhaps never will."

Corvello put the empty glass under the counter, then continued, "You must remember Madruga was not a special person. Like all of us, he knew little English, spoke it full of mistakes, was the subject of laughter by those of us who understood and should have known better. He, too, was called a fish eater, and worse names than that; but he didn't care. He paid what he owed by the only means he knew and this meant working like a horse. Now he leaves his name on the tax rolls of our county, a hard-working man who never forgot the poor land of his birth."

The men in the pool hall began to leave. They must go home, eat a bite and then sleep a little until milking time.

Mr. Freitas drove over to the ranch a week or so after the funeral.

"I could have asked you to come into town," he said to Ana and Luis, "but I couldn't resist taking another look at the cattle." He smiled. "That is, if you don't mind, and after we have discussed the business of the will. . . ."

After a proper pause he said, "Tomé Madruga was a fine man, wasn't he?"

"He was like a father to us," Ana said. "God knows, we gave him a few bad moments. What is sad, we never quite made up for it. He passed on so fast."

"Took me in, a greenhorn, taught me all he knew, gave me a start," Luis said.

The lawyer smiled. "In a way, you'll continue doing exactly what he wanted you to. For instance, the share of the land you bought. To pay for it, you'll be busy for the next twenty years. Where will the payments go? No problem here. You'll make them to the order of The Whaling Institute of the Azores. This, I know, will surprise you. You see, the old man wanted

163

this money sent over there yearly. He said, 'We have to help those poor, worthy people; send them enough for boats, harpoons, lines, telescopes. Those people should be assured a decent living, at least for a while.'"

They were sitting in the kitchen, and Mr. Freitas drank a glass of yellow milk from a Jersey cow, selected by Luis for home use. "Now," the attorney continued, "the last half of the dairy and all the cash is to be Ana's. The remaining land is also to be hers, during her natural life and to go to your son, on condition that you both marry. Naturally, you may do so at any time now, considering that Linhares is dead."

"Yes," Ana agreed.

"Madruga wanted you to be safe at all times," Mr. Freitas continued, "He used to talk to me about this whenever he came to the office. 'Nothing must happen to hurt this girl,' he used to say. I think the coming of your son was the most wonderful event in his life. After that he was ready to go. All his property was in good hands: he had an heir and that was enough."

The lawyer waited a moment. "I think he wanted to go the way he did. 'No bed for me,' he used to say. 'Who wants to give a lot of trouble to people?'" He paused. "He named Mr. Silveira as executor of his will and on his passing, Romano's bank. Be in court with me next Monday so that the will may be filed for probate."

After he had gone, Ana walked in the yard, carrying the baby in her arms.

It was midmorning and for once the work on the ranch was slackening. The fields had been irrigated a week before; it had taken Luis three days and three nights. Again, the young alfalfa covered the ground, a rich, dark green.

They were leaning against the lane fence, the child between them. "We could see the priest tomorrow, marry as soon as possible," Ana said.

"We must," Luis agreed. "Besides, we have our son to baptize."

"Why, by all means, Tio would have liked it that way."

Luis nodded, his arm about the child, holding it with Ana. Then he said quietly, almost whispering, "Little one, there will be a lot for us to do now and in years ahead. But it won't matter as long as we do it together, your mother and I, and yes, you, too, at the proper time. That is how grandfather would have wanted it."

Ana nodded silently, her lips moving in prayer. Somehow, she felt Madruga's presence, and all was better because of it.

The End

Other Titles in the Portuguese in the Americas Series